The Summer Romance of the Duke

A REGENCY NOVELLA

TRISHA FUENTES

The Summer Romance of the Duke
Copyright © 2024 by Trisha Fuentes
All rights reserved.

Book Cover and formatting provided by Trisha Fuentes
https://bit.ly/m/trishafuentes

No part of this book may be reproduced in any form or by any electronic or mechanical means, including information storage and retrieval systems, without written permission from the author, except for the use of brief quotations in a book review.

Published by

Ardent Artist Books

www.ardentartistbooks.com

About Ardent Artist Books

➥ ABOUT US

Ardent Artist Books was established in 2008

We publish modern and historical romances once a month!

Get Your FREE List: Published & Upcoming Books
visit our website at:
https://bit.ly/3Wva4o0

* * *

➥ WE HAVE BOOK TRAILERS

Follow us on YouTube!
https://bit.ly/3W3xn7a

Like, Subscribe & Comment

* * *

➥ WE HAVE SERIALIZED FICTION!

Visit our website today to download one of our stories that unfold in bite-sized pieces!

Each installment is just 99¢!

https://bit.ly/3LsDpJL

* * *

➥ LET'S CONNECT!

Fuel your love of fiction with exclusive content and captivating insights from Ardent Artist Books. Whether you crave the thrill of modern narratives or the timeless elegance of historical fiction, our newsletter delivers a curated selection straight to your inbox. Plus, as a welcome gift, receive a FREE downloadable eBook:

"The Family Fix"

https://bit.ly/49BR3UB

Contents

Chapter 1	1
Chapter 2	15
Chapter 3	31
Chapter 4	51
Chapter 5	67
Chapter 6	81
Chapter 7	99
Chapter 8	113
Chapter 9	129
Chapter 10	151
Chapter 11	169
Chapter 12	179
Chapter 13	189
Epilogue	201
The Surprise Heir	215
Service Daughter Series	217
About Trisha	221
Also by Trisha Fuentes	223

One

The grand ballroom of the Messingham estate shimmered under the flickering chandeliers, casting a warm glow upon the elegantly dressed guests who swirled like a living tapestry. Lady Juliana Langdon stepped inside, her heart racing as she took in the scene. The air was thick with laughter and the sweet strains of a string quartet, but all that filled her mind was one singular thought: Reggie.

Her sparkling blue eyes darted across the crowd, scanning the myriad of silks and satins for a familiar figure. There he was—Lord Reginald Haine, the Duke of Messingham—standing tall amidst a throng of admirers, his dark hair and piercing green eyes unmistakable even from a distance. He was engaged in lively conversation, laughter dancing on his lips, yet it did nothing to quell the fluttering in her chest.

With determination, she began to weave through the sea of finery. She maneuvered past a group of giggling debutantes, their parasols twirling idly above their heads, and sidestepped an exuberant gentleman whose bowtie threatened to pop off with excitement. Each step brought her closer, and with each passing moment, the festive atmosphere faded into a mere backdrop for her singular pursuit.

"Do excuse me," she murmured, her voice firm yet polite as she slipped past a cluster of ladies, their eyes glimmering with envy. They regarded her with a mixture of admiration and disdain, but Juliana was impervious to their scrutiny, her gaze fixed unwaveringly on Reggie.

His laughter rang clear, a sound she had longed to hear—a melodious echo of shared childhood memories. The world around her blurred; the gilded frames, the polished marble floor, the swirling gowns—all diminished until only he remained, standing like a beacon in the midst of chaos.

"Reginald," Juliana breathed, a smile unfurling across her lips as she took in the familiar contours of his face. The world around them faded into a mere backdrop, a swirl of silks and lace, but here, in this moment, they stood at the axis of their shared history.

"Lady Juliana," he replied, his voice resonating with warmth, an echo of the camaraderie forged in the innocence of youth. His green eyes, alight with mischief, met hers with an intensity that made her heart flutter. They did not need words to speak of what lay unvoiced between them—a promise suspended in the air, fragile yet unwavering.

"Have you been avoiding me, or is it simply my imagination?" She tilted her head, feigning a pout, though delight danced within her gaze.

"Ah, the weight of social obligation does conspire against us," he said, his tone light yet edged with sincerity. "But fear not; I am at your disposal for this evening."

At that, the strains of the orchestra filled the ballroom, a lilting waltz that beckoned couples to the polished marble floor. With a deftness born of familiarity, he extended his arm toward her, and she accepted it without hesitation, the subtle electricity sparking between them.

"Shall we?" he intoned, guiding her gently into the throng of dancers.

As they stepped past the thrumming crowd, Juliana felt the rhythm of the music pulse through her. Each note seemed to align with the quickening of her heartbeat, every step drawing her closer to him. Together, they glided across the marble, their movements fluid, seamlessly entwined as if choreographed by fate itself.

In those moments, lost in the dance, she could feel the whispers of the ton, the flutter of curiosity brushing against the edges of her consciousness. Yet, none of it mattered. Not the envious gazes from other ladies nor the murmurs of suitors eager to capture her attention. All that existed was the exquisite intimacy of their shared space.

"Tell me," he murmured, leaning slightly closer, the warmth of his breath grazing her ear, "what is it you desire most tonight?"

"To remain as we are," she whispered back, her pulse racing as their bodies swayed in perfect harmony. "A moment stolen from time."

"Then let us savor it," he promised, his grip on her waist tightening just enough to ground her amidst the swirling chaos of the ballroom.

And as they twirled beneath the crystal chandeliers, laughter and music enveloping them, Juliana surrendered to the intoxicating thrill of their connection. In this fleeting embrace of melody and movement, she clung to the hope that perhaps this night would be the catalyst for everything she yearned for —an unbreakable bond forged in the crucible of their hearts.

As the final notes of the waltz faded into a gentle hush, Juliana and Reggie stepped apart, the energy of their shared rhythm lingering in the air like an unspoken promise. The ballroom around them pulsed with laughter and conversation, yet it felt muted, as if the world had narrowed to include only themselves.

"Do you suppose the duke's extravagant display of peacocks on the lawn is meant to outshine his guests?" Juliana ventured, her blue eyes sparkling with mischief as she glanced toward the grand windows where the ill-fated birds strutted with all the pride of royalty.

Reggie's lips quirked into a knowing smile, his green gaze glinting with appreciation for her wit. "I daresay, if he were truly ambitious, he'd have them recite poetry as well," he replied, his tone light yet edged with sincerity. "Perhaps that would elevate this affair beyond mere spectacle."

"Ah, but poetry recited by peacocks? A most intriguing thought." Juliana laughed softly, relishing the banter that flowed effortlessly between them. "What a delightful scandal that would ignite—imagine the ton's reaction when they discover that avian artistry has eclipsed their own."

"Indeed! I can already hear Lady Pembrum gasping into her fan, feigning a swoon as she declares it a breach of etiquette." His voice dipped into mock seriousness, and Juliana could hardly contain a chuckle at the mental image.

"How positively dreadful!" she exclaimed, placing a hand dramatically upon her heart, her laughter ringing like music amidst the chatter surrounding them. "I must warn you, my lord, should a peacock take up the mantle of poet, it may inspire my own verses. I fear they would be far too risqué for polite society."

"Then let us keep your talent hidden from public view," Reggie teased, leaning closer, his breath warm against her ear, "for such scandal might render you the toast of the season, and I would rather not share you with the masses."

Juliana felt a flutter in her chest at his words. They stood at the edge of the dance floor, surrounded by swirling gowns and dapper coats, but they existed within a bubble of intimacy, each playful exchange deepening the connection that tethered them together.

"Is that jealousy I detect, my lord?" she challenged, arching an eyebrow playfully. "Surely, as the Duke of Messingham, you are accustomed to having admirers aplenty."

"Jealousy?" He scoffed lightly, though there was a spark in his eyes that suggested otherwise. "Not of those insipid suitors. My concern lies solely with your happiness."

"Such noble sentiment!" she countered, her teasing tone buoyed by the warmth of their camaraderie. "You flatter me, but do not think I am so easily swayed by flattery alone."

"Nor am I blind to the charms of my competition," he replied, his gaze drifting across the ballroom, landing momentarily on a group of eager gentlemen, all vying for a chance to capture Juliana's attention. Then, as if pulled by an invisible thread, his eyes snapped back to her, igniting the space between them anew. "But tell me, what does Lady Juliana truly desire, aside from escaping the clutches of the ton?"

"Freedom, perhaps," she mused, her voice lowering to a conspiratorial whisper. "The freedom to choose whom I wish to engage with—to dance not simply through the evening but through life itself."

"Then let us seize this night, shall we?" Reggie proposed, a flicker of determination crossing his face. "We may not be able to sway the whims of others, but we can certainly craft our own story amidst the cacophony."

"Indeed," she replied, her heartbeat quickening as they began to navigate through the throng of elegantly dressed guests, their laughter and fervent exchanges lighting the path ahead. As they moved, Reggie held her arm with the utmost care, guiding her through the sea of silks and satin, ever mindful of her comfort.

With every word they exchanged, every fleeting touch, the atmosphere crackled with something electric, both thrilling and terrifying. Juliana knew that beneath the laughter and the clever repartee lay a deeper longing—a yearning for something more than mere companionship.

The music swelled, a lively waltz that filled the grand ballroom of the Messingham estate with vibrant energy. Juliana felt the pulse of the melody in her veins as she and Reggie spun through the crowd, their laughter mingling with the notes, an effortless symphony of companionship.

"Look there," Reggie said, nodding toward a group of ladies draped in silks of the most extravagant hues. "I believe they are discussing the latest scandal involving Lord Wexley's unfortunate misadventure at the opera."

Juliana raised an eyebrow, her lips curling into a teasing smile. "Pray tell, was it not simply his propensity for dramatic flourishes? One would think he were auditioning for the stage rather than courting respectability."

Reggie's laughter rang out, drawing curious glances from nearby guests. Their banter flowed easily, like the waves lapping against the shore, and whispers began to ripple through the ballroom—a mixture of admiration and envy, underscored by the unmistakable intrigue of a bond so palpable.

"How delightful to see such ease between you two," a lady nearby remarked, her tone laced with envy, eyes narrowing ever so slightly. "It is as though you are the only ones in this room."

"Indeed," another chimed in, glancing between them with feigned innocence. "One might wonder if intimacy has blossomed into something altogether more enchanting."

Juliana felt a flush rise to her cheeks, but she held firm, diverting her gaze back to Reggie. His green eyes sparkled with mirth, yet beneath that charm, she sensed a shared understanding—a tether that bound them, impervious to the prying eyes of the ton.

"Let them whisper," Reggie said softly, leaning closer, his breath warm against her ear. "What matters is our dance, unencumbered by others' notions and expectations."

"Ah, but how can I ignore the suitors who flock like moths around a flame?" she replied, her voice steady despite the fluttering in her heart. "They are relentless in their pursuit, while I stand here entranced by a mere friendship."

"Merely friendship?" Reggie echoed, his expression shifting to one of mock incredulity. "I daresay the warmth of your smile could ignite a thousand hearts."

"Then let them burn," she said, meeting his gaze head-on, the conviction in her voice reflecting the yearning within her. "For my heart yearns for more than what they can offer; it seeks the thrill of authenticity."

As the music swirled around them, Juliana became acutely aware of the distance between them, both thrilling and agonizingly close. The other gentlemen vying for her attention blurred into insignificance, their attempts at conversation falling flat before the electric connection she shared with Reggie.

"Promise to lead me away from the watchful eyes," she teased, her heart racing at the prospect of being swept away by the very man who had captured her thoughts since childhood.

With a firm grip, he pulled her onto the dance floor, and the world around them faded into a blur of colors and sounds. As they danced, the whispers of the ton grew louder, but all the noise faded into a distant hum compared to the intoxicating connection they shared. In that moment, wrapped in the security of each other's presence, Juliana dared to dream of what lay beyond the confines of societal expectations.

Reggie's arm slipped around Juliana's waist as they navigated the throng of elegantly clad guests, his presence a steady anchor in the vibrant sea of colorful gowns and sparkling jewels. The soft murmur of conversation was punctuated by laughter, yet it felt as if the world had narrowed to just the two of them, a cocoon woven from familiarity and unspoken desire.

"Do you see how they look at us?" Reggie murmured, an amused glint in his piercing green eyes as he guided her past a cluster of ladies, their envious gazes trailing like shadows. "As though we might be plotting some great scandal."

Juliana stifled a laugh, her heart fluttering at the playful tone. "Perhaps we are," she replied, leaning closer, her breath teasingly warm against his ear. To the onlookers, they were merely friends, but beneath their playful banter lay something more profound—an intimacy that seemed to elude the prying eyes of the ton.

"Then let us give them something truly scandalous to ponder," he suggested, his voice low, laced with mischief. His fingers brushed against hers for the briefest moment, igniting a spark that sent heat rushing through her, leaving a trail of warmth along her skin.

"Only if I get to choose the scenario," she countered, her cheeky smile daring him to play along. She felt emboldened by the connection they shared, emboldened enough to push the boundaries of their friendship.

"Very well, I am at your service," he replied with a mock bow, his grin widening, exposing a flash of charm that drew admiring glances from nearby ladies.

As they continued to weave through the crowd, Juliana couldn't help but notice the subtle shifts in attention around them. Ladies in feathered hats, bright silks, and shimmering pearls cast furtive glances, their expressions a mix of curiosity and envy. They whispered behind delicate lace fans, speculating how one simple gesture could command so much admiration.

"Tell me, my lord," Juliana said, feigning seriousness as they paused near a gilded column, "do you find delight in provoking jealousy among the masses?"

"Only when it involves your company, dear lady," he replied, his gaze unwavering, filled with sincerity that made her pulse quicken.

"Ah, but the stakes are high," she teased, tilting her head with a playful flick of her auburn locks. "What if one of those jealous ladies decides to take action? I cannot bear the thought of a duel over mere flirtation."

"Let them try," he quipped, his smirk deepening, a glimmer of bravado lighting his features. "In truth, I have no intention of sacrificing our moments for the trivial pursuits of others."

"Moments, yes," she mused, holding his gaze, her heart thudding in rhythm with the music that floated through the air. Each note echoed her unspoken desires, creating a melody that resonated within her very soul.

"Perhaps we ought to steal away to the gardens, where the moonlight can cloak us from prying eyes," he suggested, leaning slightly closer, his breath mingling with hers.

The invitation hung heavy in the air, laden with promise and danger. Juliana felt the weight of expectations pressing down upon her—the expectations of family, society, and the rigid rules that dictated her every move. Yet all of that faded into insignificance beneath the intensity of Reggie's gaze, the allure of what might await them beyond the ballroom's gilded walls.

"Lead on, then," she breathed, her heart racing at the prospect of slipping away from the watchful eyes of the ton, even for just a moment. With a gentle tug, Reggie guided her away, their fingers entwined as they danced through the festivities, the world around them blurring into a haze of colors and delightful chaos.

The whispers of the ton, laced with intrigue, flitted around her like moths to a flame.

"Have you seen how Messingham watches her?" A lady in a lavender gown leaned toward her companion, her voice tinged with envy. "It is as if they are the only two souls in this grand ballroom."

Juliana felt the heat rise to her cheeks, though she maintained her composure, her auburn waves shimmering under the crystal chandeliers. She caught sight of Reggie across the floor, his dark hair tousled just so, green eyes glinting with mischief as he engaged effortlessly with a group of admirers. Each laugh he shared seemed to draw more attention to their undeniable connection, igniting curiosity among the onlookers.

"Indeed," another voice chimed in, barely concealing its disdain, "one would think they were betrothed. Yet neither has committed to any other suitors."

There it was—an unspoken truth that twisted within Juliana's chest. They had danced this intricate waltz for years, yet tonight felt different. The air crackled with an electricity that hinted at something deeper than mere friendship. As if sensing her gaze, Reggie turned and their eyes met, a fleeting moment suspended in time. His smile was both reassuring and provocative, promising secrets yet to be shared.

"Shall we?" he beckoned, offering his arm once more. They slipped away from the gathering, deftly maneuvering through a sea of silk and satin, laughter echoing behind them, while the world faded into a blur of opulence.

"Do you hear them?" Juliana asked, her voice low, yet laced with playful exasperation. "They speak as if we are but characters in a scandalous play."

"Perhaps we are," Reggie replied, an amused glimmer in his eye. "But let us not provide them with more fodder."

As they found refuge in a quiet corner, the noise of the ballroom dulled into a distant hum. They stood close, faces illuminated by the soft glow of candlelight, their breaths mingling in the tension that hung between them. Time stretched, allowing the weight of unspoken words to settle over them like a fine mist.

"Your birthday approaches, does it not?" he ventured, studying her intently.

"Yes," she admitted, her heart racing. "And yours, too. Yet here we stand, still unclaimed, despite the many eligible suitors."

"Perhaps we are waiting for something more," he murmured, his voice a velvet whisper that sent shivers down her spine. The moment felt fragile, laden with the significance of what lay ahead—a choice that loomed over them like a dark cloud, threatening to burst forth at any moment.

"Or someone," she added, emboldened by the intimacy of their secluded space.

"Someone indeed." His gaze locked onto hers, revealing depths of longing and vulnerability that belied his charming facade.

As the last notes of the evening's waltz echoed through the ballroom, Juliana felt the world narrow to just the two of them—their shared understanding swirling in the air, palpable and electric. The gathering outside continued unabated, oblivious to the tempest brewing within their hearts. In that dim corner, they stood on the precipice of decision, knowing well the path they must choose—or risk losing one another forever.

Two

A fortnight had scarcely passed since the last gala at the Messingham Estate, yet here it was again, alight with a fervor that could all but set the chandeliers ablaze. The grand ballroom burgeoned with the crème de la crème of society, each lady and gentleman arrayed in finery that whispered of wealth and whispered louder of status. Men boasted coats of deep velvets and crisp linens, while women's gowns billowed like blossoms in a zephyr, silks, and satins catching the light in a kaleidoscope of color.

The air thrummed with the strings of a quartet tucked discreetly beneath a floral bower, their melodies weaving through the throng of guests. Laughter tinkled above the music, punctuated by the clink of crystal and the rustle of taffeta. Here, in the heart of this splendid revelry, the elite of Regency England cavorted under the watchful gaze of oil-painted ancestors.

Yet beneath the surface gaiety, a current of expectation hummed. Servants, more privy to the whispers of their masters than perhaps they ought, moved with knowing glances between them. Guests, too, were not immune; their murmurs skated along the edges of conversation, speculation ripe as summer fruit.

"Have you heard? Messingham is to make an announcement," divulged a dowager countess, her voice barely contained within the confines of discretion.

"Indeed? One can only surmise the nature of it," replied her companion, a baron whose eyes betrayed a keen interest despite his measured tone.

"Matrimonial prospects, I wager," chimed in a spinster aunt from behind her fan, the words laced with intrigue. "Mark my words, some fortunate damsel is on the cusp of a most advantageous match."

With every exchange, anticipation coiled tighter, a spring wound to its utmost before the inevitable release. And at the epicenter of these conjectures stood the Duke of Messingham, blissfully unaware of the tempest he was about to unleash upon polite society.

Lady Juliana Langdon, her auburn tresses a cascade of gentle rebellion against the strictures of the evening's coiffure, wove through the throng with a grace that belied her inner tumult. Her blue eyes, usually alight with mirth or curiosity, now betrayed an introspection as she exchanged pleasantries with peers and matrons alike. The laughter and nods she offered were but shadows of her usual vivacity; her thoughts ensnared by the enigma that was the Duke of Messingham.

"Charming night, is it not, Lady Juliana?" inquired Lord Ashford, his smile expectant as he presented a glass of ratafia.

"Indeed," she replied, the word more reflex than sentiment. "The Haines always set a splendid table." Her gaze flickered past him, toward the grand staircase where Reggie was rumored soon to appear.

"Look at them," whispered Lady Beatrice, sidling up beside Juliana with a conspiratorial gleam in her eye. "The lot of them prancing about like peacocks, all for naught once Messingham's intentions are declared."

Juliana masked her disquiet with a sip of her drink. "And what if they're not what we think?"

"Come now," her friend countered with a sly tilt of her head. "You and I both know the tune that's played long before the musicians take their bow."

A heavy silence settled over the room as all attention swerved to the top of the marble staircase. There stood Reggie, resplendent in his black tailcoat and crisp white cravat, catching every eye with the dimpled charm that so often graced his lips. His posture, impeccable as the lines of his suit, hinted not at the storm he was about to summon forth.

"Esteemed guests," Reggie began, his voice carrying effortlessly above the hushed crowd. "I find myself grateful for your presence this evening, and I must beg a moment of your time for a personal indulgence."

The collective breath of the assembly seemed to pause, held captive by his announcement's prelude. Juliana's heart, a traitorous drum against her ribs, matched the cadence of anticipation that rippled through the room.

"Your moment is ours, Reggie," called out a jovial baronet, breaking the tension momentarily as chuckles fluttered through the gathering.

"Ever generous," Reggie acknowledged with a nod. "In truth, it is a matter of some import I wish to share—a declaration that will chart the course of my future, and perhaps touch upon the lives of some here tonight."

Juliana felt the words as one might feel the first droplets of an impending deluge. He had not glanced her way once, yet each syllable seemed a lodestone, drawing her spirit toward an unseen precipice. She braced herself, the crystal in her hand a cold anchor to reality as she prepared for the torrent that would follow.

"After much contemplation," Reggie continued, his demeanor a mask of resolve that belied the flicker of uncertainty in his emerald eyes, "I am pleased to announce my engagement to Lady Meredith St. Clair."

Time twisted, stretching the moment into an eternity as the words hung in the air, laden with an unthinkable weight. Juliana's breath caught in her throat, a silent gasp that felt more like a shattering. The world around her dimmed; laughter faded into a muted echo, and the glimmer of chandeliers became mere blurs of light.

"Lady Meredith?" whispered a nearby matron, her voice heavy with surprise. "How unexpected!"

"Indeed! I had thought..." another guest trailed off, their brows knitted together in confusion.

Juliana stood frozen, her pulse quickening as she fought to comprehend the reality that had just been woven before her. The sinking feeling in her heart transformed into an ache that radiated outward, pinching at her very core. Memories of shared laughter and stolen glances with Reggie flooded her mind, each one now laced with the bitter sting of betrayal.

Around her, the guests erupted into murmurs—some congratulatory, others tinged with disbelief. A knot formed in her stomach as she perceived the curiosity etched on their faces, their eyes darting between the newly engaged couple and herself, eager for scandalous revelations.

"Such an intriguing turn of events," a dandy remarked, adjusting his cravat with a flourish. "Who would have thought our dear Messingham would choose Lady Meredith? Quite the catch!"

"Well, it is obvious why he would," another chimed in, casting a sidelong glance at Juliana. "The Langdon heiress has yet to secure a match."

"Ah, but what of her friendship with him?" came a smooth voice, barely concealing its delight. "One must wonder how she feels about this news."

Juliana's cheeks burned under their scrutiny, the whispers encasing her like a web of gauzy silk. She forced her features into a semblance of composure, though inside, her heart felt like a quagmire. *How could he do this? How could he stand there, so regal, while shattering everything they once held dear?*

As she stole a glance at Reggie, his gaze was locked upon Lady Meredith, who stood radiant beside him, her smile a perfect blend of triumph and grace. The sight twisted Juliana's insides, making her feel both invisible and exposed, adrift in a sea of emotions no one else could fathom.

"Congratulations!" someone called out, the cheer ringing hollow in Juliana's ears. She willed herself to move, to act, but her limbs felt weighted by the gravity of loss. Each heartbeat echoed like a thunderclap, threatening to drown her beneath the tide of her own despair.

Lady Juliana inhaled sharply, her breath hitching as she approached Lady Meredith. The ballroom swirled around her, a kaleidoscope of silks and jewels, yet all she could see was the radiant figure before her—the woman who had just claimed Reggie's heart. With each step, she fought to maintain the polished facade that society expected from her, forcing a smile that felt brittle on her lips.

"Lady Meredith," she intoned, her voice steady despite the tempest raging within. "Congratulations on your engagement." The words tasted foreign, bitter like unripe fruit, but they slipped from her mouth with practiced ease.

"Thank you, dear Juliana!" Lady Meredith replied, her eyes sparkling like the diamonds adorning her neck. "Isn't it simply splendid? I can hardly believe it myself!" Her laughter rang out, bright and carefree, as though she were unaware of the storm swirling in Juliana's chest.

Juliana's heart sank further at the sound. *How could she feign joy when everything inside her screamed otherwise?* Each word exchanged felt like daggers, piercing through the delicate fabric of her composure. She could almost hear the muted whispers of the other guests—those prying eyes dissecting every interaction, scrutinizing her carefully crafted mask.

"Of course, it is," she managed, her smile unwavering. Yet, beneath the surface, a torrent of emotions threatened to break free. **Duty.** She was Lady Juliana Langdon, a beacon of propriety, a daughter of society. *But what of her desires? What of the laughter shared with Reggie, those stolen moments that lingered like sweet wine upon her tongue?*

How can he choose her?

The question gnawed at her as she forced herself to engage in idle chatter, her mind a cacophony of conflicting thoughts. *He must be aware of the bond we share. He must remember our dreams, whispered beneath the stars!* Yet here she stood, watching him bask in another's light, feeling small and invisible beside the splendor of their union.

"Are you well, my dear?" Lady Meredith's voice pulled Juliana from her spiral.

"Quite well," she replied with a practiced smile, though her heart drummed a frantic rhythm against her ribcage. *I must not appear weak,* she chastised herself. *I must uphold my honor, even if it means sacrificing my happiness.*

As she continued to converse, her mind drifted back to Reggie —the warmth of his gaze, the way his laughter sparked joy within her. It was then that doubt seeped into her resolve. *Did he truly understand the gravity of his choice? Had he thought of her at all while making such a life-altering decision?*

But inside, her heart twisted. *What am I to do now?* The weight of expectation pressed down upon her shoulders, an anchor dragging her deeper into a sea of despair. Torn between societal obligation and her yearning for Reggie, she felt the first cracks in her veneer.

With every polite exchange and forced smile, the distance grew, a chasm filled with unacknowledged feelings and regrets. And yet, as she stood there amidst the glittering throng, a flicker of rebellion ignited within her. *Why should I not fight for what I desire?* But the question loomed heavy—a reminder of the choices she had to make, choices that would define the rest of her life.

"Lady Juliana, are you listening?" Lady Meredith's voice danced in the air, but it faded into the background as she wrestled with the swirling chaos within.

"Forgive me," she murmured, her smile wavering for just a moment. In that fleeting instant, she caught sight of Reggie across the room, his laughter mingling with the music—a haunting melody that echoed her own longing.

"Of course," Lady Meredith said, oblivious to the turmoil brewing beneath Juliana's calm exterior.

And so, she smiled again, though this time it felt more like a mask than a reflection of true emotion. *Let them think what they will*, Juliana thought fiercely, her heart pounding as her resolve began to crystallize. *I shall reclaim my happiness, no matter the cost.*

"Reggie," Lady Juliana's voice cut through the ambient chatter, her heart racing as she moved toward him. The grand ballroom of the Messingham Estate shimmered with crystal chandeliers, casting a glow that seemed to mock her inner turmoil. She caught a glimpse of Lady Meredith, radiant and poised, surrounded by admirers. The sight twisted in her chest like a dagger.

"Juliana!" Reggie's expression shifted from joviality to surprise, his green eyes widening at her approach. He stepped away from a cluster of gentlemen, their laughter fading into an echo as he focused solely on her. "What is it?"

"Could we speak... alone?" Her words were laced with urgency, the polite smile she wore faltering under the weight of her request.

"Of course." He glanced back at Lady Meredith, who appeared engrossed in conversation, then turned his full attention to Juliana. Unassuming, he followed her to a quieter alcove draped in satin and adorned with delicate flowers—an expanse of tranquility amidst the ball's vibrant chaos.

"Is something amiss?" Reggie asked, his brow furrowed slightly, oblivious to the storm brewing within her.

"Amiss?" Juliana echoed, her pulse quickening. The very word felt inadequate to convey the tumult roiling in her heart. *How could I possibly explain this anguish?* "No, nothing is amiss, but—" She hesitated, choosing her next words with care. "I must know what you are feeling about your announcement."

"Ah, yes, my engagement to Lady Meredith." He ran a hand through his dark hair, a hint of sheepishness creeping across his handsome features. "It has stirred quite the excitement, has it not?"

"Excitement?" Her voice rose slightly, betraying her calm facade as she fought to regain control. "I daresay it has caused quite a stir indeed, but what of your own feelings? This decision—" She paused, her throat tightening. "It is a significant one, is it not?"

"Significant, yes, but also right," he replied, confidence lacing his tone. "Lady Meredith is charming, and it is time for me to settle down. My family expects it."

"Your family expects it," Juliana repeated, her voice now barely above a whisper, tinged with disbelief. *But what do you expect, Reginald?* "And what of your own heart? Does it not play a part in this?"

"Juliana," his gaze softened, yet remained untroubled. "You know how society works. A man must make decisions grounded in reason."

"Reason." The word stung; it hung between them, heavy with unspoken implications. Juliana took a breath, striving to maintain her composure. "Do you truly believe that love can be weighed against societal expectations?"

"Love is important, of course, but…" His voice trailed off as if he had not fully considered the ramifications of his own proclamation.

"Yet here we stand, discussing duty instead of desire." She clenched her hands, the urge to grasp onto his arm almost overwhelming. "Do you not feel even a flicker of regret?"

"Regret? No, Juliana." His response was immediate, but there was a shadow crossing his expression. "I want what is best for everyone involved."

"Everyone except yourself," she murmured, her heart sinking further. *How could he dismiss this?* "You deserve happiness, Reggie, not merely compliance to tradition."

"Perhaps," he conceded, glancing to where Lady Meredith laughed, her melodious sound drifting through the air. "But happiness takes many forms. It is time I embrace the life set before me."

"Embrace or endure?" Juliana countered, a tremor in her voice. "You do not have to settle for anything less than true joy, my lord."

"Joy comes with responsibility, Juliana." His words were firm, though the flicker of uncertainty in his emerald eyes told another story.

"Then let us redefine what that responsibility entails." Her conviction surged, battling the despair that threatened to overwhelm her. "You may choose a path that allows you to seek your own desires."

"Juliana..." He hesitated, and in that moment, she saw the flicker of doubt she had longed for. But before she could grasp it, he continued, "I appreciate your concern, but I must consider the future."

"Yes, the future," she echoed, her voice steadying despite the tempest within. "A future without the chance of discovering true love."

"Perhaps this is love, in its own way." His expression was earnest, but she could see he wasn't truly convinced.

"Perhaps, but it feels hollow when there is more at stake."

"More?" He tilted his head, the confusion evident. "Juliana, I—"

"Never mind," she interrupted, forcing a smile that felt brittle on her lips. "I only wish you happiness, Reggie. Truly."

"Thank you," he said, still searching her face for meaning.

"Now, go," she urged gently, her heart breaking with each word. "Lady Meredith awaits your attention."

"Very well." He nodded, still looking uncertain, and with a final glance, he turned to rejoin the lively crowd.

Alone once more, Juliana leaned against the cool wall, the warmth of the ballroom now suffocating. *Why was it so easy for him to deny what lay between them?* Her chest tightened, and the mask she wore threatened to shatter.

Lady Juliana turned away from the bustling ballroom, her heart in disarray. The laughter and music felt distant, as if she were submerged beneath the surface of a turbulent sea. She moved toward an alcove draped in rich velvet, seeking refuge from the prying eyes and inquisitive minds that thrived within these gilded walls.

As she leaned against the cool marble, memories flooded her thoughts—Reggie's infectious laughter during their childhood escapades, the stolen moments beneath the old oak tree where they once declared their everlasting friendship. In those innocent days, they had forged an unspoken pact, one that promised a future entwined together, unburdened by societal pressures.

But how naïve we were, she mused bitterly. *The world has no patience for such whims.*

"Juliana?" His voice reached her before she could mask her turmoil. She turned to find Reggie, his expression earnest yet confounded. He found her. He found her, hiding. "You seemed lost in thought."

"Just contemplating the evening," she replied, forcing a lightness into her tone that felt like a brittle façade. "It is quite the spectacle, wouldn't you agree?"

"Yes, splendid indeed." He stepped closer, concern etching deeper lines upon his brow. "Are you well? You seem... unsettled."

"Unsettled?" She laughed softly, betraying none of her internal storm. "How could I be? It is merely a ball, after all."

"Yet you do not seem as joyful as usual." He studied her, and she fought the urge to look away. "Is it the announcement that troubles you? I understand this may be difficult news."

"On the contrary, I am thrilled for you," she asserted, but the words twisted in her throat. *Thrilled? How can I even say that when my heart is splintering?*

"Thank you. That means a great deal coming from you." There was a sincerity in his gaze, but it only deepened her despair. *He does not see me—not really.*

"Reggie," she began, her voice trembling slightly, "do you ever consider what might have been?"

"Consider what?" He tilted his head, genuine confusion painted across his handsome features. "I know there are expectations, but I believe Lady Meredith will make a fine wife."

"Expectations," she echoed quietly. The word hung in the air between them like a specter. "And what of our own dreams? Our pact?"

"Juliana, that was childish folly." He chuckled lightly, but she detected a hint of discomfort. "We were young, and the world was… different."

"Was it?" Her heart raced; anger mingled with sorrow. "Or did we simply will ourselves to ignore the truth—the truth that we shared something profound?"

"Profound?" His brow furrowed further, his green eyes searching hers. "It was friendship, nothing more."

"Friendship," she repeated, each syllable heavy with implication. "If that is all it was, then why does it ache so deeply now?"

"Because you care for me," he said gently, though he seemed unaware of the full extent of her feelings. "And friends care for one another. It's natural."

"Natural," she whispered, letting the word hang in the air as she stared at the floor, willing the tears to stay hidden. *What if it is more than that? What if I am meant to fight for my happiness?*

"Juliana, I must go," he murmured, glancing over his shoulder toward the ballroom where Lady Meredith awaited. "I cannot keep her waiting."

"Of course," she responded, the weight of resignation suffocating her resolve. "You should go."

"Will you be alright?" he asked, concern etched on his face, but she merely nodded, unable to articulate the tempest within.

"Yes, perfectly well." As he walked away, she felt the finality of the moment settle around her like a shroud.

Alone once more, Juliana's composure crumbled. She stepped from the alcove into the dim corridor, needing distance from the revelry that felt mocking now. Outside the grand estate, the cool night air enveloped her; she inhaled deeply, allowing the chill to soothe her heated cheeks.

Fight or yield? The question reverberated through her mind. Should she claim the love that had always lingered just beneath the surface, or should she adhere to the societal expectations that bound them both?

As she leaned against the cool stone wall, the stars twinkled above, indifferent to her plight. With a quiet sob escaping her lips, she let the tears flow freely for the first time that evening.

Three

A WEEK LATER

The grand ballroom of the Barnham Estate shimmered under the glow of crystal chandeliers, their light casting an ethereal sheen upon the polished marble floor. Lady Juliana Langdon stepped inside, her mother's gloved hand resting lightly on her arm, but it was as if a weight had settled upon her heart. The chatter of the assembled guests swirled around her like a distant melody, and yet, her focus narrowed to a singular pursuit: to find Reggie.

"Juliana, dear, do look at those exquisite gowns," her mother remarked, gesturing towards a group of ladies adorned in vibrant silks. But Juliana's gaze remained fixed, scanning the room until she finally spotted him—Reggie.

A sudden pang twisted in her chest as she beheld him standing with Lady Meredith St. Clair, their heads bent together, laughter mingling with the music that filled the air. His dark hair gleamed under the opulent chandeliers, and his green eyes sparkled with mirth, captivating not only Lady

Meredith but the entire assembly. Juliana felt her breath hitch; there was a tenderness to their interaction that sent a jolt of despair through her.

"Look at how they laugh," whispered a voice in her mind, cruelly reminding her of the bond she once shared with him. She forced herself to swallow the painful lump in her throat, straightening her shoulders with a resolve she hardly felt. A smile, practiced and polite, formed on her lips, concealing the turmoil beneath.

"Shall we move closer?" her mother urged, oblivious to Juliana's internal struggle.

"Not just yet," Juliana replied, her words steady despite the tempest within. The last thing she desired was to intrude upon the scene before her, a tableau of affection that felt both familiar and utterly foreign. She could not bear the thought of disrupting their moment, nor allowing her own emotions to spill forth like rain upon a sunlit day.

Instead, she stood rooted, her heart heavy with longing, pondering the years spent together in mischievous childhood escapades, the laughter they had shared, and the secrets exchanged in hushed whispers. *How had they arrived at this juncture?*

"Come now, dear," her mother said, urging her forward. Yet Juliana remained still, her feet seemingly bound by an invisible thread. The space between them felt insurmountable as if a chasm had opened where once there had been camaraderie.

Why must he choose her? The thought flared hot within her, unwelcome but undeniable. Juliana inhaled deeply, drawing strength from the elegant surroundings, determined to master her sorrow. One more glance, she told herself. Just one.

She allowed her gaze to drift back to Reggie, who caught her eye for a fleeting moment—a heartbeat suspended in time. But as quickly as it had sparked, he returned his focus to Lady Meredith, the warmth of their shared laughter wrapping around them like a cloak. Juliana felt the breath escape her, a whisper of resolve fading into the air.

"Very well," she murmured softly, her heart sinking further. With a slight nod to her mother, she turned away, unwilling to show any sign of weakness. In that moment, she comprehended the bitter truth: she must accept this new reality, even if it meant walking a path lined with unspoken heartache.

Juliana took a step into the grand ballroom, the soft rustle of her silk skirts whispering against the polished floor. The air was thick with the scent of roses and candle wax, punctuated by the lilting strains of a string quartet weaving through the cacophony of laughter and conversation. She forced her chin high, a practiced smile gracing her lips as she scanned the sea of opulent gowns and dapper waistcoats.

"Juliana, dear, do try to engage," her mother's voice cut through the din, nudging her forward with gentle insistence.

"Of course, Mama," she replied, though her heart sank further with every step that brought her closer to Reggie and Lady Meredith. They lingered in a corner, their heads inclined towards one another, oblivious to the world around them. Each shared laugh felt like a dagger lodged firmly in her chest.

"Lady Hargrove, how lovely to see you!" Juliana greeted a middle-aged woman adorned in emerald green. The older lady beamed, her cheeks flushed with pleasure, and they exchanged pleasantries that danced on the surface—compliments about the evening, inquiries about health—all while Juliana's mind remained tethered to that corner.

"Have you heard of the new opera coming to London? I believe it features the renowned tenor from Italy," Lady Hargrove continued, oblivious to Juliana's distraction.

"Ah, yes," Juliana said, nodding politely. But her eyes flickered back to Reggie, whose laughter rang clear and bright, accompanied by the dulcet tones of Lady Meredith. In that moment, the room faded, and all Juliana could hear was the echo of their joy.

"Juliana, dear," her mother interjected once more, breaking the spell. "Come along now."

Before she could protest, her mother led her through the throng of elegantly attired guests, each step a battle against the tumultuous emotions roiling within her. As they approached the couple, dread coiled tighter in her stomach. *What would she say? How could she disguise the turmoil boiling beneath her composed facade?*

"Messingham! Lady St. Clair!" her mother called out, her voice bright with false cheer. Juliana's breath hitched as she came to stand before them, the warmth of their intimacy striking her like a sudden chill.

"Good evening," Reggie's voice reached her, laced with an easy charm that had always disarmed her. She forced herself to meet his gaze, where genuine affection sparkled in those piercing green depths. For a moment, the world narrowed to just the two of them, but the weight of Lady Meredith beside him pulled Juliana back to reality.

"Lady Juliana, what a pleasure!" Lady Meredith's melodious tone filled the space, cutting through Juliana's reverie. She offered a smile that glistened with confidence, unaware—or perhaps unbothered—by the tension thickening the air.

"Indeed, a pleasure," Juliana managed, her voice steady despite the tempest within. She took a deep breath, plastering on a polite smile that would not betray her heartache. There was no room for weakness here; she must uphold the ideals of friendship and decorum, even as the sight of them together threatened to unravel her composure.

"Quite the list of guests this evening," Juliana said, her voice a soft note above the din of the ballroom. The words rolled off her tongue with practiced ease, as if rehearsed in her mind a thousand times. She forced her lips into a polite smile, though beneath the surface, her heart twisted painfully at the sight of the newly engaged couple.

Lady Meredith clasped her hands together, golden tresses shimmering under the crystal chandeliers. "It is quite the season for celebrations, is it not?"

"Indeed." Juliana nodded, a mere flicker of warmth igniting her chest, quickly extinguished by the chill that gripped her heart. She studied Lady Meredith, whose poise and charm would enchant any man. How effortlessly she radiated happiness, how blissfully unaware of the storm brewing within Juliana.

"Reggie must be overjoyed," she added, her eyes darting to him, drawn like a moth to a flame. He stood beside Lady Meredith, tall and confident, his dark hair framing a face that had always been a source of comfort in her childhood. With a charming smile, he turned towards her, their gazes colliding for a heartbeat—a silent exchange laden with unspoken memories.

"Ah, yes! I have never seen him so animated!" Lady Meredith's laugh was light and airy, a sound that danced across Juliana's skin like an unwelcome breeze. "His joy is infectious, wouldn't you agree?"

"Most certainly," Juliana replied, the words tasting bitter on her tongue. She felt the flutter of apprehension tighten in her throat, threatening to spill forth the torrent of emotions she had so carefully guarded. As she glanced back at Reggie, who met her gaze with that same disarming smile, she quickly averted her eyes, unwilling to betray herself.

"Your kindness means the world to us, dear Juliana," Reggie said, his voice warm yet distant, as if he sensed the fragile thread that held them together was fraying. It pained her to see him so close yet feel an abyss stretching between them, one forged by his choice and her unyielding loyalty to friendship.

"Of course," she murmured, forcing the weight of her truth down into the depths of her heart. A fleeting moment passed where the noise of the ballroom faded, leaving only the echo of unspoken words hanging in the air. She willed herself to remain steady, a pillar of grace in this tempest of feelings.

"Now, do tell me about your latest endeavors," Lady Meredith interjected, drawing Juliana back to the present. Each syllable was sweet, yet laced with a tension that made Juliana acutely aware of the sharp contrast between their worlds.

"Ah, there are none worth mentioning," Juliana deflected smoothly, the practiced elegance of her tone betraying nothing of her inner turmoil. "I remain devoted to my duties at home."

Lady Meredith smiled brightly, but Juliana could not meet her gaze again; it was a reminder of everything she wished to conceal. Instead, she focused on the dance of silks and satins around her, longing for the solace of solitude even amid the thrumming life of the ballroom.

"Tell me, Reggie," Lady Meredith's voice chimed, each word carefully crafted. "Have you given any thought to our plans for the upcoming soirée at the Whitmores?"

"Ah, the Whitmores," Reggie replied, his tone light yet tinged with an undercurrent of seriousness, as if assessing the weight of the question. His green eyes sparkled, but Juliana could not help but detect something deeper lurking behind that charm. *Was it merely the flicker of candlelight playing tricks on her heart?*

"One can hardly resist the allure of such a gathering," Juliana interjected, forcing a smile that felt like a fragile mask. "The entertainment they promise is often quite diverting." She glanced sideways, desperate to gauge Reggie's reaction, her pulse quickened with anticipation.

"Diverting indeed," Lady Meredith agreed, her soft laughter merging with the thrumming music of the ballroom. Juliana's chest tightened. The sound was sweet, yet it felt like a siren call beckoning her into uncharted waters.

"Though I must confess," Reggie continued, tilting his head slightly, "I find myself more intrigued by the company than the spectacle itself." He cast a glance in Juliana's direction, his gaze lingering just long enough to ignite a flicker of hope within her—was there a hint of longing behind those emerald depths?

"How delightful to hear!" Lady Meredith responded, her expression brightening. "You flatter us both, but surely you jest." Her laughter was light, yet Juliana caught the subtle tightening of her lips; a veneer of confidence expertly masking her awareness of their dynamic.

"Not jesting at all," Reggie countered, his tone earnest. "In truth, I have always appreciated spirited discourse over mere entertainment."

"Then we shall consider ourselves fortunate," Juliana replied lightly, her voice steady despite the turmoil in her heart. She scrutinized him closely, searching for any flicker of uncertainty, a momentary falter that might betray his feelings about this engagement. But his demeanor remained resolute, exuding confidence that only deepened her sense of dismay.

"Lady Juliana," he began, his attention shifting fully to her, "what do you make of the recent whispers regarding the

Duke's estate? They say the renovations are nothing short of extravagant."

"Extravagant may be an understatement," Juliana replied, her mind racing to keep pace with the conversation, even as her heart clamored for acknowledgment of its silent ache. "However, I believe it speaks to the ambition inherent in noble pursuits. One must remain ever vigilant against complacency in society," she added, her words laced with a wisdom borne from watching the world around her.

"Wise words, as always," Reggie complimented, and for a fleeting instant, she allowed herself to bask in the warmth of his praise. Yet, beneath the surface, she sensed a chasm widening, the very foundation of their friendship shifting as Lady Meredith reclined closer to him, her laughter tinkling like glass.

"Speaking of ambition," Lady Meredith chimed in, her tone teasing, "have you considered what your own future holds, dear Juliana? Surely a lady of your grace and intellect has suitors aplenty?"

"Only the most determined of them," Juliana replied, maintaining her composure. Inside, however, she wrestled with the pang of longing that throbbed insistently. She did not wish to dwell upon her own prospects when Reggie loomed so near, splendidly engaged to another.

"Such modesty! You ought to accept every invitation with open arms," Lady Meredith urged, her voice mellifluous and persuasive. Yet Juliana barely heard her words; her focus remained fixed on Reggie's expression, which had turned thoughtful, perhaps even pensive.

"Indeed, Juliana," Reggie said slowly, seemingly lost in contemplation. "Your presence is a treasure to any gathering."

"Ah, flattery will get you nowhere, my lord," she quipped lightly, though the fluttering in her stomach betrayed her. She observed him closely, searching for even the slightest hint of doubt in his eyes—something, anything, that might suggest he too felt the weight of this engagement.

"Perhaps it's time you allowed yourself to be pursued, then," he replied, a teasing glimmer returning to his gaze.

"Perhaps," she echoed, her heart heavy with a truth she could not voice. As their banter continued, she shielded her emotions behind a polite façade, her thoughts whirling like the dancers twirling around them. Each laugh, every shared glance, solidified the distance between them—a space where friendship once flourished now marred by unfulfilled desire.

"Ultimately, it is one's choice," she managed, her voice crisp. Yet with each passing moment, she feared that choice had already been made, leaving her stranded on the shores of longing while Reggie sailed toward a new horizon.

"Art and literature?" Reggie interjected, a hint of disbelief coloring his tone. "I dare say, you could hold the attention of a ballroom full of admirers if you chose to grace them with your presence."

"Ah, but what is a ballroom without genuine affection?" Juliana countered lightly, her gaze flickering to Reggie's face for a moment too long. She noted the way his brow furrowed slightly, an uncharacteristic shadow crossing his features. "Besides, I find it far more entertaining to delight in your engagement," she continued, redirecting the conversation with deftness. "Tell me more of how the two of you intend to spend your first months together as man and wife."

Lady Meredith clapped her hands together, a childlike glee illuminating her expression. "We have plans for a grand tour of the continent! It will be splendid, don't you think? Just imagine the sights we shall see!"

"Splendid indeed," Juliana echoed, though the word tasted bittersweet on her tongue. Each detail shared was like a dagger buried deeper within her heart, twisting with every mention of their future. Her mind raced, searching for another diversion. "And what of your families? Have they expressed their thoughts on your journey?"

"Of course," Lady Meredith replied, waving a dismissive hand. "They adore Reggie, and I am certain they would support any venture he wishes to embark upon."

"How fortunate you are," Juliana said softly, her heart aching at the thought of her own family's expectations. "May I suggest that you also take time to explore the local culture? There is great beauty in tradition, after all."

"Maybe we shall!" Reggie remarked, a glimmer of enthusiasm returning to his eyes. Yet, beneath that charm lay a flicker of uncertainty that Juliana clung to desperately.

"Speaking of traditions," Juliana ventured, hoping to divert the focus once more. "Have you considered how you will celebrate your wedding? The season is ripe with opportunities."

"Why, yes! We've discussed the possibility of a grand ball," Lady Meredith gushed, her voice rising with each word. "Imagine the splendor!"

"Indeed," Juliana murmured, feeling the conversation slip further from her grasp. As the topic swirled around her, she felt the walls of the ballroom closing in.

"Juliana," Reggie prompted, his gaze lingering on her a heartbeat longer than necessary. "You ought to join us in planning; your taste is renowned, after all."

"Alas, I fear I must excuse myself," she interjected, her voice firm despite the tremor beneath. "I believe I see Lord Pembrum in need of greeting. You know how much he enjoys discussing his collection of—"

"Of course, we shan't keep you!" Lady Meredith chimed in, waving her off with a cheerful disposition.

"Do enjoy your evening," Juliana managed, offering a polite smile before making her escape.

As she retreated to a quiet corner of the ballroom, the orchestral melody faded into a distant hum. Here, away from the laughter and light, she drew a breath, allowing the noise to dull to mere echoes. Her heart still thudded with the remnants of their conversation, but here, in the shadows, she could gather herself.

She tucked a stray lock of hair behind her ear, the familiar gesture betraying her inner turmoil. What had once been effortless banter now felt like a tightrope walk, each step perilous and fraught with emotion. To support Reggie was a privilege, yet the cost weighed heavily upon her spirit. Steeling herself against the onslaught of feelings, she allowed the scene before her to fade into the background, determined to maintain her dignity amidst the chaos of her heart's desires.

* * *

THE MUSIC SWELLED, but to Juliana, it was mere background noise. She leaned against the cool marble balustrade, her heart constricting as she pinched her eyes shut. A tear escaped, trailing a path down her cheek—a betrayal of the composure she had so carefully maintained throughout the evening.

"Why now?" she whispered to herself, the words escaping like a breath held too long. "Why must my heart be so treacherous?" Each drop that fell felt like an echo of the laughter she had just left behind, a reminder of the joyous scene in which she could never fully partake.

How could she be so foolish? A lifetime of friendship with Reggie had prepared her for many things, but not this: not the sight of him with Lady Meredith, who wore his affection like a shawl, warm and enveloping. Their engagement was announced with such fervor, such celebration—how could she have thought she would remain untouched?

"Control yourself, Juliana," she scolded softly, wiping the remnants of her weakness with the edge of her glove. The silk was unforgiving, but she pressed on; the tears were insistent, each one a testament to the ache of unspoken feelings. "You are not a child anymore."

"Support him," she urged inwardly, the mantra rising to the surface. "You will support him. It is what he deserves." But the weight of that resolve bore down upon her, pressing against her chest as though it might suffocate her spirit. How could she stand by while her heart shattered silently in the shadows?

"Alone again," she murmured, glancing around the vast ballroom. The opulent chandeliers cast a golden glow over the revelers, yet she felt adrift, a solitary figure amidst a sea of jubilance. Her fingers trembled as they brushed against the delicate lace of her gown.

"Do not let them see you falter," she reminded herself. "You are Lady Juliana Langdon." The title felt both a comfort and a burden. With every breath, she steeled her resolve anew, willing the darkness to retreat.

Taking a deep breath, she straightened her spine, allowing the elegance of her upbringing to flow back into her demeanor. She dabbed at her eyes, ensuring no trace of her emotional tempest lingered. "I shall support him," she repeated firmly, tasting the bittersweet promise on her lips. "Even if it means cloaking my own heartache in silence."

With determination ignited within her, she rejoined the throng of guests, stepping back into the light of the ballroom, her facade restored. Each smile she wore was a shield, her laughter a weapon against sorrow. Lady Juliana would navigate this world with grace—her heart may ache, but her loyalty would never waver.

With a firm resolve, Juliana stepped back into the ballroom, her heart pounding beneath layers of silk and satin. The strains of a waltz enveloped her, a lively melody that felt at odds with her inner turmoil. She adjusted her posture, lifting her chin slightly as she approached a cluster of guests gathered near the refreshment table.

"Lady Juliana!" called out Lady Clementine, her voice bright and cheerful, drawing the attention of several nearby gentlemen. "What a delight to see you! Have you danced yet tonight?"

"Not yet, my lady," Juliana replied, forcing a smile that belied the ache within. "I am merely enjoying the spectacle." Her eyes darted momentarily toward Reggie, who stood with Lady Meredith, their laughter ringing like chimes in the air. Each peal struck her heart, but she turned quickly, masking her sorrow.

"Come now, we must remedy that!" Lady Clementine insisted, tugging at Juliana's arm. "How can one attend such a splendid ball and not partake in its pleasures?"

"Perhaps a dance, then," Juliana acquiesced, allowing herself to be swept into the fray. As the music swelled, she moved gracefully, her steps light but purposeful. The swirling skirts of her gown brushed against her legs, a reminder of the elegance she wore like armor.

"Tell me, dear Juliana, have you heard the news?" Lady Clementine continued, her eyes sparkling with mischief.

"Lord Hargrove is quite taken with you. I daresay he may propose before the season concludes!"

"How flattering," Juliana replied, her tone polite yet distant. The notion of romantic entanglements felt like a far-off land, unreachable while reality anchored her firmly in place.

"Flattering indeed, though I suspect your heart lies elsewhere," Lady Clementine teased, a knowing glimmer in her gaze. Juliana swallowed, her pulse quickening as she flicked another glance at Reggie, still ensconced in Meredith's company.

"Ah, well, my heart is a fickle thing, is it not?" she deflected, a practiced lightness coloring her voice. "I prefer to focus on friendship, for it is far more reliable."

"Indeed, but do not deny the charms of romance entirely," Lady Clementine smiled, nudging her companion playfully. "You might just find yourself dancing with Lord Hargrove after all!"

"Perhaps," Juliana murmured, her thoughts drifting away again. She watched as Reggie leaned closer to Lady Meredith, his eyes alight with affection—a sight that twisted her insides anew. Yet she held her mask steady, feigning interest in the idle chatter surrounding her.

"Who else has caught your eye this evening?" Lady Clementine pressed, oblivious to Juliana's distraction.

"All are equally delightful," Juliana replied, keeping her tone bright. "It is an enchanting gathering, is it not?" The words fell from her lips, rehearsed and polished, but they did little to fill the void where her hopes lay buried.

She stole another glance at Reggie, whose laughter mingled with that of Lady Meredith, an effortless bond that stung like a thorn. Would he ever look at her with such warmth? Would he even notice if her heart broke right there amidst the glittering lights?

"Juliana, dear, join us!" came a call from Lord Pembrum, beckoning her over with a wave. With a deep breath, she turned her back on the couple, burying her feelings beneath a layer of social niceties.

"Of course, my lord," she replied, stepping forward with grace. Each movement was deliberate, a careful choreography designed to conceal the tempest of emotions roiling within. She laughed and engaged in light conversation, each word a shield against the longing that threatened to unravel her composure.

Yet, even amid the merriment, she could not help but glance back toward Reggie and Lady Meredith. Their chemistry was palpable, an unspoken connection that made her heart ache deeper with every fleeting moment. She would remain loyal; she would uphold their friendship, no matter the cost.

"Do you not agree, Lady Juliana?" Lady Clementine's voice broke through her reverie, pulling her back to the present.

"Indeed," Juliana responded, forcing her attention back to the gathering around her. "A splendid evening, truly." But as she spoke, her mind lingered on the couple across the room, a silent witness to their joy, cloaked in the guise of a friend.

"Juliana!" called out another acquaintance, interrupting her reverie. She turned away, engaging in trivial conversations about the latest gossip—the impending nuptials, rumored scandals—while her mind played tricks on her heart, twisting within like a coiled spring. Each laugh, each soft whisper shared between Reggie and Lady Meredith ignited her resolve, but it also stung with an almost unbearable sharpness.

"Such a charming affair, is it not?" Lord Pembrum remarked, gesturing toward the dance floor, yet Juliana's attention was ensnared once more by the sight of Reggie's captivating green eyes—eyes that had always held a touch of mischief and warmth, now directed at his fiancée with a sincerity that dashed against her carefully constructed walls.

In that fleeting moment, their gazes locked across the sea of silks and satin, and time seemed to suspend itself. The noise of laughter, the clinking of glasses, faded into a distant hum. It was just he and she, the years of friendship weaving themselves into an unspoken bond, a thread fraying at the edges, yet still holding firm.

"Lady Juliana?" The voice of Lord Pembrum broke the spell, pulling her back to reality. With a start, she realized the depth of what she had seen reflected in Reggie's eyes—a spark of something genuine, something intimate. Panic surged through her, quickening her pulse.

"Forgive me," she murmured, the words barely escaping her lips. She looked away, averting her gaze as if the act could shield her from the truth of her own heart. He would be happy. That was the vow she had made to herself, the promise of unwavering support. Even amidst the ache that threatened to swallow her whole, she refused to falter.

"Do you wish to join us for the next dance?" Lord Pembrum continued, blissfully unaware of the internal turmoil brewing within her. She nodded, forcing a smile that felt more like a mask than a reflection of her spirit.

"Of course, my lord. I would be pleased." But as they moved toward the center of the ballroom, her heart lingered in that brief connection, hidden beneath layers of propriety and grace.

With every twirl and spin, the ache remained, yet so did her resolve. For within the depths of her quiet despair lay a fierce loyalty—a determination to support Reggie, even if it meant sacrificing her own desires. As the music swelled again, she swallowed hard, pushing her pain deeper, ready to uphold the facade of friendship until the final note faded away.

Four

Juliana burst into the drawing room, the heavy door swinging against the wall with a resounding thud. The scent of lavender wafted through the air, mingling with the faint crackle of the fire that flickered in the hearth. She cast a quick glance around the opulent space, seeking the familiar comfort of her sister, Lady Beatrice, who sat gracefully on a damask chaise, her brow furrowed in concern.

"Juliana, dear," Beatrice said softly, her voice a balm against the turmoil swirling within her sister's heart. "What troubles you so?"

Without pausing to respond, Juliana began to pace, her shoes tapping lightly on the polished floorboards. She wrung her hands together, her fingers twisting and turning as if they could somehow unravel the knots tightening in her chest. Each step felt weighted, her mind racing faster than her feet could carry her.

"Beatrice!" she exclaimed, halting before her sister, the anguish in her sparkling blue eyes cutting through the warm glow of the drawing room. "It is all utterly insufferable! How can one man possess such power over my well-being?"

"Juliana," Beatrice said gently, leaning forward, her warm brown eyes locked onto her sister's. "You must speak plainly. I cannot help you if you do not share your burden."

Juliana resumed her restless pacing, the soft rustle of her gown echoing the tumult of her thoughts. "I feel adrift, as though I am but a leaf caught in a tempest," she muttered, her voice strained. "The world expects me to remain silent, to accept what is thrust upon me without question. But how can I? How can I simply allow this... this engagement to unfold?"

Beatrice rose from her seat, her composure unwavering despite Juliana's evident distress. She moved to intercept her sister, placing a steadying hand on Juliana's shoulder. "You are not bound by the expectations of society alone," she said, her tone firm yet tender. "You have the right to pursue happiness."

A shiver passed through Juliana, the warmth of Beatrice's touch grounding her momentarily. Yet, even as her sister's words wrapped around her like a silken shawl, doubt crept back in. "What if my desires lead to ruin?" she whispered, her voice cracking under the weight of her fears. "What if I lose everything I hold dear?"

"Then we shall face it together," Beatrice replied, her grip tightening ever so slightly, her resolve an anchor for Juliana's stormy soul. "But first, you must confront your own heart. What do you truly wish for?"

The fire popped, sending a shower of sparks up the chimney, mirroring the sudden flare of hope igniting within Juliana. Her breath caught in her throat as she met her sister's gaze, searching for answers amid the chaos. In that moment, standing there in the elegant drawing room, the vast expanse of their family estate surrounding them, she realized that perhaps, just perhaps, she was not as powerless as she had believed.

Juliana halted mid-pace, her heart racing like a horse in full flight. She turned to face Beatrice, the weight of unspoken words pressing heavily upon her chest. "Reggie," she began, her voice barely above a whisper, trembling as if it held the very essence of her turmoil. "He is to be wed to Lady Meredith." The words tumbled forth, laced with anguish as they hung in the air, heavy and suffocating.

Beatrice's brow furrowed in concern, her warm brown eyes widening with understanding. "I see," she replied softly, urging Juliana to continue with a gentle nod.

With a quick intake of breath, Juliana resumed her restless movement, her fingers entwining in the loose strands of her hair. "I cannot comprehend how he could choose her when…" Her voice faltered, caught between desire and despair. She cast a glance toward the window, where the late afternoon sun filtered through the delicate lace curtains, casting a patchwork of light across the room. "How can he be so blind?"

"Blindness is not always a choice, dearest sister," Beatrice interjected, her tone soothing as she leaned forward slightly. "What is it that you feel?"

Juliana paused, her thoughts swirling like autumn leaves caught in a tempest. "I have loved him for what seems an eternity," she confessed, her heart pounding fiercely against her ribcage. "Yet, my affection remains shrouded in silence, for I am but a spectator to his happiness with another."

"Ah, but perhaps you are not merely a spectator," Beatrice said, her voice imbued with a quiet strength. "You hold power over your own heart."

"Power?" Juliana echoed incredulously, a bitter laugh escaping her lips. "What power do I possess? In this world of propriety, I am but a pawn, subject to the whims of fate and societal decree." Her gaze dropped to the ornate carpet beneath their feet, a tapestry of fortunes woven into intricate patterns, each thread a reminder of the constraints binding her.

Beatrice's expression softened further, a maternal warmth emanating from her very being. "You possess the ability to act, dear sister. You may choose to speak your truth to Reggie, even amidst the chaos of expectation."

"But what if he spurns me?" The tremor in Juliana's voice betrayed her fear, her hands now clenched tightly at her sides.

"Then you will know," Beatrice replied firmly, her emphasis on 'know' echoing in the drawing room. "To remain in uncertainty is a torment far worse than the sting of rejection."

Juliana inhaled shakily, her mind wrestling with Beatrice's counsel. "And if I pursue him, how can I reconcile my desires with the expectations laid upon me?" A wellspring of emotion surged within her, threatening to overflow.

"Your desires are no less valid than society's expectations," Beatrice assured her, her gaze unwavering. "You must listen to your heart. What does it truly yearn for?"

As Juliana searched her sister's face for encouragement, the flickering flames in the fireplace seemed to mirror the tumult of her soul. "It yearns for Reggie," she admitted, each syllable laden with both hope and trepidation. "But what would become of us both should I dare to follow such inclinations?"

"That is for you to determine," Beatrice replied, her voice steady as a lighthouse guiding a ship through stormy seas. "Trust in the bond you share. In love, there lies a bravery that transcends all else."

Juliana's heart fluttered at her sister's words, yet the path ahead remained shrouded in uncertainty. She felt the weight of her choices pressing down, but with it came a glimmer of resolve. Perhaps, just perhaps, she might find the courage to confront the tempest brewing within her heart.

Juliana's fingers danced nervously along the edge of the mahogany side table, glancing at the fine porcelain clock that ticked steadily, each chime resonating like a reminder of her own unrelenting turmoil. The drawing room felt both stifling and sanctuary, its elegant decor contrasting with the chaos brewing within her heart.

"Beatrice," she began, her voice trembling as she turned to her sister, "what if I pursue him? What if I dare to reveal my feelings?" She swallowed hard, the weight of her confession pressing against her chest. "The thought of rejection is... unbearable."

Beatrice's gaze softened, understanding etched across her features. "You are not alone in this struggle, dear sister. Fear can be a formidable foe, but it must not dictate your choices."

Juliana inhaled sharply, her thoughts racing. "But what of the consequences? Society deems love a mere transaction—a game of power, not passion. Should I defy their expectations, I risk becoming an outcast, perhaps even losing Reggie altogether."

"Your heart speaks a truth that society cannot fathom," Beatrice replied, her tone unwavering like a steady anchor amidst a storm. "To deny yourself the right to love is to imprison your spirit. You owe it to yourself to explore these feelings."

As Juliana's resolve wavered, Beatrice reached across the space between them, her hands enveloping Juliana's. The warmth of her sister's touch offered solace, grounding her tumultuous thoughts. "What do you truly desire? Let your heart guide you."

Juliana felt the gentle squeeze of Beatrice's hands steadying her, an unspoken promise that she would not navigate this path alone. Tears threatened to spill, but she blinked them away, focusing instead on her sister's steadfast expression. "I long for him, Beatrice," she admitted, her voice barely above a whisper. "Yet the fear of facing rejection—of being cast aside while he commits to another—it paralyzes me. I am trapped between longing and propriety."

"Then let us confront that fear together." Beatrice's eyes sparkled with determination, her grip firm. "It is vital to be honest with yourself about your true feelings. Do not let societal norms dictate your life's narrative."

Juliana's breath caught in her throat, the gravity of her sister's words settling heavily upon her. It was not just a question of what society would think; it was a matter of her own happiness, her own desires. She looked down at their interlocked hands, feeling the strength that pulsed through Beatrice's fingertips and into her own trembling palms.

"Perhaps," Juliana mused, her voice steadier now, "the only way to discover my heart's intent is to confront this situation head-on. I cannot remain in this limbo, forever yearning for what might have been."

"Exactly," Beatrice affirmed, a proud smile warming her features. "You possess an inner strength that could rival any societal constraint. You will not be silenced by fear."

With newfound clarity, Juliana squeezed her sister's hands in return, feeling the flicker of courage ignite within her soul. The path ahead remained fraught with uncertainty, but with Beatrice by her side, she felt emboldened to take her first steps toward reclaiming her heart from the clutches of doubt.

Juliana's breath hitched as she gazed at the delicate porcelain figurines lining the mantelpiece, their painted faces frozen in serene expressions. The very stillness mocked her turmoil, and she felt the sting of tears welling in her eyes. "But what if I am not enough?" The words escaped her lips like a whisper, trembling with the weight of her fear.

Beatrice tightened her grip on Juliana's hands, her warm brown eyes filled with a fierce protectiveness. "You are more than enough, dear sister. Love is not bound by the constraints of society; it flourishes when two souls are brave enough to embrace it."

"Yet I feel so small," Juliana confessed, wiping away a stray tear that escaped down her cheek. The flickering candlelight cast shadows across the drawing room, amplifying her sense of isolation amidst the opulence surrounding them. "Reggie is engaged to Lady Meredith. What hope do I have?"

"Hope thrives in the most unlikely of places," Beatrice replied, her voice steady as the rhythmic ticking of the clock echoed in the silence. "Remember our bond, Juliana. We have faced trials before, and we shall face this one together."

"How can I confront him? If I reveal my heart, I risk everything—the scandal, the whispers." Her voice cracked again, fear spilling forth like a fragile vase teetering on the edge of a table.

"Perhaps it is time to stir the pot a little," Beatrice suggested, a glint of mischief dancing in her eyes. "What if you invented a suitor? A dashing gentleman from abroad—someone who would rouse Reggie's curiosity and perhaps even jealousy."

Juliana blinked, the notion taking root in her mind. "A suitor?" she echoed slowly, her pulse quickening at the idea. "To gauge his intentions?"

"Precisely! Use this fabrication as a means to draw out his true feelings," Beatrice urged, her enthusiasm illuminating the dim room. "It would place you in a position of power rather than helplessness. You deserve to know if he truly cares."

"Could such a ruse work?" Juliana mused, the corners of her mouth lifting slightly despite herself. For the first time, a flicker of excitement pushed against her trepidation.

"Trust in the strength of your resolve," Beatrice replied softly, her gaze unwavering. "He must see you for the treasure you are, and if that requires a bit of deception to reveal his heart, then let us devise a plan worthy of a novel."

Juliana pondered her sister's words, the warmth of Beatrice's faith wrapping around her like a comforting shawl. "I must consider this carefully," she said, her voice steadier now. "But I no longer wish to remain stagnant. I want to fight for my heart."

"Then let us begin forging your path," Beatrice declared with renewed vigor, a smile breaking through the tension. "Together, we shall create a tale that will leave Reggie questioning everything he thought he knew."

"Yes!" Juliana's pulse quickened. The thought of Reggie, so accustomed to being the sole object of her affection, suddenly confronted with the idea of rivalry, filled her with a heady exhilaration. "He must be made to realize what he risks losing."

"From Belgium, then?" Beatrice mused, tapping her chin as her mind whirred with possibilities. "Or perhaps a man of

French nobility, returned to reclaim his ancestral estate? We could name him…"

"Henri!" Juliana interjected, her brow furrowing in concentration. "Henri de Beaumont, an elusive gentleman with ties to the court. It is both exotic and intriguing."

"Perfect," Beatrice affirmed, her smile broadening. "Now, we shall need letters—the kind that speak of admiration from afar. Your suitor will possess such charm that it will draw even the most steadfast heart into a whirlwind of jealousy."

Juliana felt a warmth blossom within her, suffusing the space where despair had lingered only moments before. "And you will help me?" she asked, a note of vulnerability creeping into her voice.

"Every step of the way, dear sister." Beatrice took Juliana's hands in hers, squeezing them gently. "You need not face this alone. Together, we shall craft your narrative, one that leaves no room for doubt in Reggie's heart. He must see you as the jewel you are, worthy of all the treasures that love can offer."

"Thank you, Beatrice," Juliana breathed, her spirits lifting like a morning mist. "With you by my side, I feel I can face anything."

"Then let us begin our preparations at once," Beatrice urged, her eyes sparkling with determination. "We have much to devise, and time is of the essence. Let us ensure that when Henri arrives, it is with a flourish that none shall forget."

With a firm resolve coursing through her, Juliana straightened her back, aligning her shoulders as if donning an invisible armor against the world. The weight of uncertainty that had previously pressed upon her heart began to lift, replaced by a flicker of audacity igniting within.

"Beatrice," she said, her voice steady and clear, "I cannot adequately express my gratitude for your wisdom and support. You are not merely my sister, but my anchor in this tumultuous sea of societal expectations." Her blue eyes sparkled with sincerity, reflecting the depths of her appreciation. "Your understanding of my plight is a rare gift."

"Juliana, you must know," Beatrice replied, her tone imbued with warmth, "that I have always believed in your strength. It is time you recognize it within yourself." She stepped closer, her presence enveloping Juliana like a soft cloak.

"How fortunate I am to have you," Juliana continued, allowing herself a brief smile amidst the gravity of their conversation. "You are both loving and cunning—a true trickster in the best sense."

"Then let us not tarry any longer!" Beatrice exclaimed, a glint of mischief dancing in her warm brown eyes. "We shall concoct our scheme with the utmost fervor! Imagine the look on Reggie's face when he learns of Henri!"

Before she could finish her thought, Beatrice pulled Juliana into a tight embrace. The familiar scent of lavender and rosewater surrounded her, offering solace as they shared a moment steeped in affection and solidarity. Juliana felt the pulse of their bond thrum louder, a testament to their unwavering love.

"Together, we can be bold," Beatrice murmured into her hair, squeezing her sister gently. "And together, we shall navigate this ruse, ensuring it is both delightful and impactful."

"Indeed," Juliana breathed, the warmth of the embrace rekindling her courage. As they released one another, she met Beatrice's gaze, determination mirrored in both their expressions.

"Let us prepare for the unveiling of Henri," Beatrice declared, her eyes sparkling with excitement. "A suitor from abroad, shrouded in tantalizing mystery. How could Reggie resist questioning his intentions?"

"Or mine," Juliana added, her heart racing at the prospect. The thrill of the challenge sent a ripple of exhilaration through her. Together, they would orchestrate this grand charade—one that held the potential to sway the affections of the man who haunted her every waking thought.

"Onward then, dear sister," Beatrice said, a conspiratorial smile gracing her lips. "The game is afoot, and our strategy shall unfold with all the elegance of a fine waltz. Let us make haste before our opportunity slips away."

The drawing room felt imbued with an electric anticipation, shadows flickering in the candlelight as if echoing the tumult within her heart. She turned toward the door, her fingers brushing against the smooth wood, feeling the solidity of her next steps beneath her fingertips.

"Remember, dearest," Beatrice called softly, her voice a gentle tether. "Your resolve is your greatest strength."

Juliana nodded, a flicker of a smile gracing her lips before she squared her shoulders and opened the door. The corridor beyond stretched out like an uncharted path, each step resonating with the cadence of her racing thoughts. The air was rich with the scent of polished mahogany and distant lavender, mingling into an olfactory reminder of home, yet now it felt charged with a new purpose.

As she walked, her mind danced with possibilities—Henri, the French suitor they had concocted, would soon become the fulcrum of their ruse. She could almost hear Reggie's voice, laced with curiosity and concern, questioning this mysterious figure who had seemingly swept into her life from afar. *Would he be jealous? Would he even care?*

The echo of her footsteps faltered for a brief moment as doubt crept in, but she banished it with a firm shake of her head. No more hesitation; she had resolved to seize her happiness. With every stride, she envisioned the encounter that awaited her. Would Reggie's piercing green eyes light up with interest, or would they cloud over with indifference?

As she approached the grand staircase, its banister glimmering under the light of the chandelier, she caught a glimpse of herself in the ornate mirror lining the wall. Her auburn hair fell gracefully around her shoulders, framing a face that displayed both vulnerability and newfound determination.

"Lady Juliana!" A voice broke her reverie. It was Mrs. Hargrove, the housekeeper, bustling past with an armful of linens. "You look positively radiant today!"

"Thank you, Mrs. Hargrove," Juliana replied, her tone steadier than she felt. She offered a polite smile, the warmth genuine despite her racing heart. "I believe I shall take a stroll in the gardens."

"Excellent idea! The roses are in full bloom," the housekeeper chirped, disappearing down the hall with a satisfied nod.

Juliana's heart quickened at the thought of the garden—a familiar sanctuary where secrets were whispered, and dreams took flight. It was there, amidst the vibrant blossoms, that she would prepare her heart for the impending confrontation with Reggie.

Pushing open the heavy door leading outside, she stepped into the sun-drenched expanse of the garden, the fragrant air enveloping her like a soft, silken shawl. Each petal seemed to shimmer with promise, the vivid colors reflecting her own swirling emotions.

"Today, everything changes," she murmured to herself, gathering her courage. With a deep breath, she began walking along the cobblestone path, letting the sound of her footsteps mingle with the rustle of leaves above.

As she approached a secluded alcove nestled among climbing roses, her pulse quickened with excitement and trepidation. She could almost envision Reggie standing there, his charming smile drawing her closer, yet she knew that first, she must establish the foundation of this elaborate charade.

"Let us see what unfolds," she whispered, her heart lighter and her mind clearer, ready to face the challenges that lay ahead in pursuit of Reggie's heart.

Five

TWO DAYS LATER

Juliana stepped through the grandiose doors of the Messingham estate, her breath catching momentarily at the sight before her. She had been invited to an intimate dinner—only fifteen guests this evening. The dining area gleamed with crystal chandeliers, their light casting a soft glow over the polished floorboards where guests twirled in elegant harmony. Yet, despite the opulence surrounding her, a weight settled heavily upon her chest.

"Ah, Lady Juliana! You grace us with your presence!" Lady Haines' voice rang out, bright and inviting, yet it only amplified the tumult within her. She offered a polite smile, but her heart was not in the performance. She scanned the room, her gaze searching for one figure amongst the sea of silk and satin.

There he was—the Duke of Messingham—his tall form commanding attention as he stood conversing with his betrothed, Lady Meredith St. Clair. The sight of them was like a dagger to her heart. Lady Meredith's golden hair shimmered as she laughed, her delicate features illuminated by the flickering candlelight. Reggie's deep laughter echoed across the room, rich and warm, an intoxicating sound that once filled Juliana with joy but now ignited a fire of jealousy within her.

"Juliana, dear, come join us!" Lady Meredith beckoned, her voice musical, yet the invitation felt like a trap. Juliana's throat tightened. She could not bear to intrude upon their intimacy. Instead, she took a step back, melding into the shadows cast by towering potted palms, her heart racing as she watched them.

Reggie leaned closer to Meredith, his green eyes sparkling with mirth. He reached out, brushing a stray curl from her face, a gesture so tender it sent a jolt of bitterness coursing through Juliana's veins. Each shared glance and soft laugh between them twisted like thorns in her heart. How could he be so carefree, so unburdened by the knowledge that another held his affections?

"Isn't it delightful?" Lady Meredith exclaimed, tilting her head in a way that made her seem ethereal, enchanting. "The way the stars glow tonight? It seems almost magical."

"Indeed," Reggie replied, his voice low and intimate. "It reminds me of our summer evenings at the lake, does it not?"

A memory surged within Juliana, unbidden—the two of them, laughing beneath the willow trees, the sun setting in hues of gold and amber. But that was a past long buried under layers of duty and expectation. Now, as she observed him anew with another woman, the pang of longing transformed into a sharp ache of despair.

"Juliana, you truly must join us!" Lady Meredith called again, her melodic tone laced with genuine warmth, yet all Juliana could hear was the distant echo of what might have been.

"Perhaps... another time," she murmured, retreating further into the shadows, watching helplessly as Reggie and Meredith continued their dance of flirtation. With each passing moment, her resolve wavered, consumed by envy and heartache. If only he could look her way, if only he could see past the glamour and the obligation that now bound him.

But they were lost in their world, a world where she could never belong. And as a soft laugh rang out yet again from Lady Meredith, Lady Juliana turned away, hoping the darkness would swallow her sorrow whole.

Lady Juliana turned from the parlor window, where she had been a reluctant spectator to the merriment below. The grand dining room of the Messingham estate buzzed with laughter and clinking crystal, yet every sound felt muffled to her ears, as if the very fabric of gaiety wrapped around her was but an illusion.

"Lady Juliana!" called out a voice that pierced through her reverie. It was Mrs. Standish, a portly matron whose penchant for gossip surpassed even her fondness for fine cuisine. "Do come, dear! We were just discussing the latest fashions from Paris."

"Ah, yes," Juliana replied, forcing a smile that felt like a mask over her true emotions. She glided towards the group, her auburn hair gleaming in the candlelight, though the warmth of the glow did little to thaw the chill settling within her heart.

"Have you seen the new silks?" Mrs. Standish continued, her eyes alight with enthusiasm. "They say the colors are vibrant enough to rival a peacock's plume!"

"Indeed," Juliana responded, nodding as her gaze flickered past the gathering. There stood Reggie, laughing at something Lady Meredith had said, his green eyes sparkling with delight. The sight sent a fresh wave of disappointment crashing against her composure, and she fought to keep her expression neutral.

"Juliana, my dear, you must speak!" Lady Beatrice interjected, concern etched on her face. Juliana could feel her sister's watchful gaze, discerning the strain in her demeanor.

"Of course, I beg your pardon," Juliana murmured, returning her attention to Mrs. Standish. "The Parisian styles do seem to evoke quite the stir." Her voice wavered slightly, betraying the tumult beneath the surface.

"Stir? Oh, they are positively revolutionary!" another guest chimed in, and the conversation surged around her like an unrelenting tide. Juliana nodded, offered polite laughter, and gestured gracefully, but inside, the battle raged on.

"Do tell us, when you make your next purchase, will it be for yourself or for... someone else?" Lady Beatrice's question hung in the air, laden with unspoken implications.

"Someone else?" Juliana echoed, her heart racing at the thought of what lay beyond mere frivolity. "Oh, I would not presume to indulge anyone with my choice. After all, there are no suitable engagements on the horizon for me."

"Quite right, dear. One cannot be too careful these days," Mrs. Standish replied, oblivious to the tremor in Juliana's voice.

A forced laugh escaped Juliana's lips, hollow and brittle like the delicate china adorning the table. Each chuckle felt like shards of glass lodged in her throat, an echo of joy that rang false against the backdrop of her despair.

"Such a lovely evening, is it not?" she declared, attempting to steer the conversation away from the piercing scrutiny of her sister's gaze. Yet, with each laugh shared amongst the guests, each resounding cheer that filled the air, the weight of her heart grew heavier, pressing down upon her chest like a lead weight.

"Yes, indeed!" Mrs. Standish exclaimed, reaching for a glass of champagne. "You simply must attend the ball next week, Juliana! What say you?"

"Of course," she replied, her voice barely above a whisper, and suddenly, she felt the room swell with laughter, the faces of acquaintances blurring into one. A storm brewed within her, and she struggled to stifle the swell of emotion threatening to consume her.

"Are you quite well, my dear?" Beatrice asked, her brow furrowed with concern.

"Perfectly well," Juliana lied, though the words tasted bitter on her tongue. With a practiced smile, she turned back to her companions, but the façade was fraying. Each moment spent pretending chipped away at her resolve, revealing the anguish hidden beneath polished elegance.

"How splendid this evening is!" she proclaimed, her laughter rising too high, too erratic, drawing curious glances. Yet, amidst their cheerful chatter, her gaze involuntarily returned to Reggie, who seemed to shine ever brighter beside Lady Meredith.

And in that moment, surrounded by gaiety, Lady Juliana felt utterly alone. She felt a sudden constriction in her throat as she stepped away from the crowd, her heart pounding beneath the layers of silk that clung to her form. The laughter and chatter faded into muffled echoes, and with each step toward the shadowed corridor, the air grew heavier, laden with the scent of roses from the nearby garden.

"Excuse me," she murmured to Lady Ashcroft, who barely registered her departure, too enraptured in a tale about a recent soirée. Juliana's fingers grazed the wall, seeking support as though the very fabric of the house might hold her together.

She swept through the ornate door leading to a secluded sitting room, the dim light casting gentle shadows on the delicate furnishings. It was here, amid the quiet elegance of embroidered cushions and polished mahogany, that she finally allowed herself to breathe. The solitude enveloped her like a thick fog, isolating her from the merriment beyond.

"Why must it hurt so?" she whispered to the empty space, her voice trembling as she sank onto a fainting couch, its upholstery cool against her skin. Her fair complexion flared with heat, a stark contrast to the chill of despair creeping over her heart. She pressed her palms against her cheeks, fighting back the tide of emotion that threatened to spill forth.

But the façade had cracked, and the overwhelming ache in her chest surged forth, shattering any resolve she possessed. Tears spilled from her eyes, warm streaks against her flushed skin, and she buried her face in her hands to muffle the soft cries that escaped her lips. Each sob echoed with the weight of unspoken words—a confession of love, longing, and loss for the man who now danced with another.

"Reggie," she gasped, the name a bittersweet balm on her tongue. Memories of their shared laughter, stolen glances, and youthful dreams swirled around her like specters, taunting her with what could have been. She trembled, not merely from the chill of the room but from the tempest within, her heart thrumming with unrequited desire.

"Why did I let this happen?" The question lingered in the air, heavy and unanswered. She longed to scream out her anguish, to shake off the chains of societal expectations that bound her heart in silence. Yet here she remained, trapped in the gilded cage of propriety, while Reggie twirled effortlessly in the arms of Lady Meredith.

As the tears flowed freely, each drop seemed to etch the pain deeper into her spirit. Lady Juliana Langdon, the epitome of grace and poise, crumpled beneath the weight of her heartache, revealing the vulnerable woman hidden beneath the veneer of elegance. And she wept, surrendering to the storm that raged within, alone in the shadows while the world continued to dance in the light.

The heavy door creaked open, and Lady Juliana stepped back into the grand ballroom, her heart racing. The laughter and chatter of the guests enveloped her like a cacophony of confusion, each cheerful note striking against the storm brewing within her. She felt exposed, as if the fabric of her dress could not shield her from the piercing gazes of those who danced obliviously to the tumult of her emotions.

She caught sight of Reggie across the room, his form tall and commanding amid the swirling gowns and fluttering fans. He stood with Lady Meredith—a vision of effortless beauty and charm—his laughter mingling with hers like a melody that made Juliana's stomach churn. Her fists clenched at her sides, nails biting into her palm.

"Why must you torment me so?" she whispered under her breath, the words laced with bitterness. It was then that a reckless impulse seized her, pushing her forward through the throng of aristocrats, each step echoing her resolve.

"Reggie!" she called out, her voice firm yet trembling. He turned, surprise flickering across his features, momentarily displacing the ease of his conversation. In that instant, time slowed; the world around them faded, leaving only the two of them suspended in an unspoken tension.

"Juliana?" His brow furrowed with concern, but she saw the glint of curiosity in his green eyes, a spark that drove her resolve deeper.

"May I speak with you?" She gestured toward the dimly lit alcove near the grand staircase, where shadows offered a semblance of privacy. A nod was all it took for him to follow, his expression shifting from surprise to apprehension.

In the alcove, the weight of their shared history loomed large, but Juliana cast it aside, desperation clawing at her throat. "I cannot endure this farce any longer," she said, her voice low but fierce enough to cut through the tension. "You need to know… I am engaged."

His face paled, confusion tightening his features. "Engaged? To whom?"

"Henri de Beaumont," she declared, each syllable heavy with defiance. "Of Belgium." The name hung between them like a boulder, crushing any lingering hope of understanding.

"Henri de Beaumont?" Reggie echoed, disbelief etched across his handsome face. "But why would you—" His words faltered, the hurt palpable in his tone.

"Because that is what is expected of me!" she shot back, anger igniting the vulnerability that had threatened to consume her moments before. "I cannot remain shackled to my own desires while you cavort with another!" The fire in her chest surged, demanding release.

"Is this what you truly want?" he demanded, stepping closer, his voice a low growl. But there was something else beneath the surface—a flicker of possessiveness that she had never seen before.

"Want? What does that even matter now?" she spat, her breath quickening. "You have made your choice clear. I will not be left to pine while you dance with your intended."

"Juliana…" He stepped back, the distance between them suddenly vast, his expression contorting into a mixture of confusion and hurt. "This engagement—it cannot be true," he murmured, almost to himself.

"Believe what you will." She swallowed hard, refusing to let her resolve waver. Yet inside, a tempest raged, her heart pleading for something more than the brittle façade she had constructed.

"How can you say that?" he pressed, his green eyes narrowing, a storm gathering within them. "You do not wish to marry him. You cannot!"

"Perhaps not. But I have no other choice!" Her voice cracked, the truth threatening to spill forth, raw and unrefined.

"Do you love him?" The question hung heavy, laden with implications that sent shivers down her spine.

"Does it matter?" she retorted, her pulse quickening, fighting against the urge to reveal the depth of her feelings. "It is done, Reginald! You must accept it."

The silence between them stretched, taut as a finely drawn bowstring, and Lady Juliana's pulse quickened with the weight of her confession. She could see the turmoil etched across Reggie's features, his brow furrowed in concentration as he grappled with the implications of her words. How easy it would be to dissolve into despair, yet beneath the tumult lay a flicker of something else—a glimmer of hope that perhaps he still cared.

"Reggie," she ventured, her voice trembling slightly, "you must know I did not speak those words lightly." Her eyes searched his, desperate for acknowledgment.

"Did you mean them?" His voice was barely above a whisper, an edge of pain lacing each syllable. "Do you truly intend to bind yourself to him?"

"Intend?" she echoed, the word tasting bitter on her tongue. "It is no longer a matter of intention, but duty." Yet even as she spoke, a part of her yearned to reach out, to bridge the chasm that felt insurmountable.

"Is that what you wish? To marry Henri de Beaumont?" The question hung heavy between them, a raw wound exposed to the chill night air.

"Wish?" She paused, swallowing back the swell of emotions threatening to overwhelm her. "What I wish is irrelevant." But in her heart, a whisper persisted: if only he would declare himself—if only he would fight for her now, when every moment mattered most.

His gaze faltered, and for a fleeting second, she glimpsed a flicker of something primal—was it longing? Jealousy? Perhaps both. It emboldened her, a heady rush coursing through her veins.

"Reggie," she pressed, stepping closer, her breath shallow, "your silence speaks volumes. You care."

"Care?" He scoffed, but the tightness around his mouth betrayed him. "You have chosen your path, Juliana. Why would my feelings matter now?"

"Because they do! At least to me." Her voice rose, fueled by conviction. "You are not merely a memory to me; you are—" She caught herself, the enormity of her unspoken truth clawing at her throat. "You are the one who holds my heart," she blurted, the words escaping before she could contain them.

A profound stillness enveloped them, the world outside fading into insignificance. Reggie's expression shifted, confusion mingling with an unmistakable hurt.

"Your heart?" he repeated, disbelief coloring his tone. "And yet you would give it to another?"

"Not willingly!" she cried, her hands trembling at her sides. "I am trapped by expectations, by society's demands. But you... you should know that I would choose differently if I could."

"Choose differently?" His voice sharpened, and the intensity in his gaze ignited a fire deep within her. "So there is a choice after all?"

"Perhaps," she murmured, emboldened by the moment. "But that choice lies with you. If you desire me—"

But before she could finish, the room swelled with tension, the air thickening around them. Reggie's silence fell like a heavy curtain, suffocating the intimacy they had created.

"Reggie," she implored, but the weight of his indecision

loomed large. He stood before her, a statue carved from uncertainty, his features unreadable.

And in that silence, her heart twisted painfully, a relentless ache consuming her. She had revealed her soul, stripped bare of pretense, yet here he remained—silent, immovable, and filled with questions left unanswered.

With every passing heartbeat, dread coiled within her. Would he ever speak? Or would they remain locked in this limbo of what could be? The uncertainty gnawed at her, leaving her suspended on the precipice of hope and despair, teetering dangerously close to the edge.

Six

Juliana stood before her mirror, steadying her breath as she scrupulously adjusted the bodice of her gown. The soft fabric of pale lavender draped elegantly over her form, its simplicity a welcome reprieve from the elaborate attire expected at every soirée in London. She tugged at the sleeves, allowing them to fall delicately down her arms, and let her auburn curls tumble loosely around her shoulders, framing her face with the ease of unpretentious beauty.

"Today, I shall be free," she whispered to her reflection, though the words felt hollow against the weight of anticipation that knotted her stomach. The countryside called to her, a siren song promising solace amidst the chaos of the season's engagements. Yet, even as she prepared to escape the confines of society, her heart thudded with the knowledge of who would accompany her. Her sister Beatrice was supposed to be her companion for the day, but at the last moment, Reggie asked if he could take her instead.

With a final glance to ensure her appearance was satisfactory, she descended the staircase, each step echoing through the quiet halls of her estate. The carriage awaited, its polished wood gleaming under the morning sun. As she approached, her gaze fell upon the Duke of Messingham, leaning casually against the side, his green eyes glinting with mischief yet shadowed by an unseen burden.

"Ah, Lady Juliana," he said, a half-smile playing on his lips. "I daresay you look positively radiant this morning."

"Spare me your flattery, Reggie," she replied, striving for lightness despite the tension swirling between them. "I trust you are not merely attempting to charm me into an agreeable mood."

"Whatever could lead you to think so?" he asked, raising an eyebrow, though the warmth in his tone betrayed him. The truth lingered unspoken, hovering just above their heads like the clouds threatening rain.

"Come now, I've known you since we were ten." Juliana's voice was firm as she stepped into the carriage, hoping to quell the stirrings of emotion that threatened to overwhelm her. The interior was adorned with plush fabrics and intricate carvings, but it suddenly felt confining, as if the very air conspired to hold her captive within its walls.

"Ready for our adventure?" Reggie inquired, his tone light but laced with an underlying tension.

"Indeed," Juliana said, forcing her own smile as she settled beside him. Though they were separated by mere inches, the distance felt insurmountable, laden with the unsaid truths that danced around them. "Although, I am quite surprised Beatrice allowed me to leave unchaperoned."

"She is quite acquainted with me, she knows I will not tarnish your reputation," Reggie laughed, getting comfortable in his seat. He knocked on the side of the driver's window.

The carriage lurched forward, jolting her from her thoughts. The rhythmic clatter of hooves against cobblestones created a percussive backdrop to their silence, and the world outside began to blur—a stream of greens and browns melding into one another as they left the city behind.

"Do you ever wonder what lies beyond the horizon?" Reggie's voice broke through the quiet, a curious spark lighting his features. "What awaits us in the countryside?"

"Perhaps a respite from the expectations that weigh us down," Juliana ventured, her heart quickening at his earnestness. How she longed to speak freely, to share the tumult within her without fear of judgment or consequence.

As the carriage rolled onward, the tension thickened, weaving itself into the fabric of their journey—a silent promise that whatever awaited them at the estate would force them to confront the truths they had thus far avoided.

The carriage came to a halt, its wheels sinking slightly into the gravel with a final, resigned sigh. Juliana hesitated for but a moment, her heart thrumming with anticipation and trepidation, before she stepped down onto the ground.

"Welcome to Windermere," Reggie announced, his tone laced

with a mix of pride and possessiveness as he gestured towards the sprawling estate before them.

Juliana's breath caught in her throat. Before her lay an expanse of vibrant colors that danced in the sunlight—a tapestry woven from the hues of blooming roses, lilacs, and daisies, each petal shimmering like a jewel. The gentle sway of the tall grass beckoned, whispering secrets only the wind seemed to understand. She felt as though she had stepped into a painting, one that promised serenity and adventure alike.

"Is it not splendid?" she murmured, her gaze sweeping across the manicured lawns that stretched endlessly toward the distant horizon, where the sky brushed against the earth with a soft blue hue.

"Indeed," Reggie replied, his own eyes gleaming with enthusiasm as he fell into step beside her. "Shall we explore?"

He moved ahead, their footsteps falling into a comfortable rhythm. As they wandered deeper into the gardens, the meticulously arranged flower beds framed their path, each bloom a testament to the care bestowed upon this estate. Juliana's fingers grazed the edges of velvety petals, relishing the tactile connection to nature she so often craved amidst the rigidity of societal expectations.

"Do you remember our childhood adventures?" he asked, his voice breaking through her reverie. "Every nook and cranny of your father's estate was a new realm to conquer."

"Ah, yes!" Juliana laughed softly. "You insisted on claiming every tree as your fortress while I played the damsel in distress. If only we had known then how foolishly romantic it all was."

"Foolish, perhaps," he conceded, a crooked smile playing at the corners of his lips, "but I would argue there was wisdom in our youthful imaginations. We were unencumbered by the weight of expectation."

"How true that is," she replied, her heart fluttering in resonance with the sun-dappled leaves overhead. Yet, beneath the lightness of their exchange lingered a heaviness—an unasked question that hung between them like ripe fruit, begging to be plucked.

As they meandered along the winding paths, the air grew thick with the scent of jasmine and honeysuckle, intoxicating and sweet. The beauty of the surroundings seemed to mirror the tumult within her, a vivid contrast to the dark clouds of her unresolved feelings towards him. His presence stirred something deep inside her, a longing that defied the constraints of propriety.

"Look there," Reggie pointed towards a small grove of trees, forming an inviting archway that led further into the estate. "Let us see what wonders await beyond."

"Lead on, brave knight," she teased, her tone light, but her pulse quickened as he took the lead, their bodies mere inches apart. The world around them faded, and for a brief moment, it was just the two of them against the backdrop of nature's splendor.

With every step, every shared glance, the lines of friendship began to blur, and Juliana found herself torn between the nostalgia of their shared past and the uncertain future looming ahead. What secrets awaited them in the depths of Windermere? And could they navigate the tangled emotions growing stronger with each passing moment?

"Reggie," she began, her voice barely above a whisper, but he turned, his expression curious yet guarded.

"Yes?" he prompted, his brow furrowing slightly as if sensing the shift in the air.

"Nothing," she replied, forcing a smile that felt more like a mask than a reflection of her heart. The estate loomed large, majestic and beautiful, yet it was the man beside her who commanded her attention, drawing her deeper into the labyrinth of her own emotions—both thrilling and terrifying, as they ventured forth together into the unknown.

"Do you suppose the flowers here possess the gift of speech?" Reggie quipped, plucking a delicate bloom from its stem and holding it aloft like a trophy.

"Perhaps they whisper secrets to one another," Juliana replied, a smile breaking across her face as she stepped closer, drawn by the glimmer of mischief in his emerald gaze. "Though I fear their confessions would be rather dull."

"Indeed! Just imagine, 'Oh, look at that dreadful weather,'" he mimicked, waving one hand dramatically. "Or, 'How unseemly it is for Lady Pembrum to sport that shade of pink!'"

Juliana laughed, the sound light and musical, momentarily dispelling the tension that had clung to them since their arrival. "You have a most vivid imagination, my lord. I daresay you should write a book on the inner lives of plants."

"An admirable suggestion! Though I fear it would not capture the attention of the ton," he replied with an exaggerated sigh. "They prefer tales of dashing rogues and star-crossed lovers."

Her breath caught slightly at his words, a warmth blooming in her cheeks. "Ah, but perhaps there is something to be said for subtlety—a narrative woven with the threads of reality."

"Subtlety has its merits, yet I suspect it lacks the flair required to captivate a ballroom full of London's finest," he teased, taking a step back as if to gauge her reaction.

"Very true; the art of spectacle reigns supreme," she conceded, though the playful air between them felt charged, every word laced with unspoken truths.

As they continued along the narrow path bordered by lush hedges, a sudden rustle in the foliage startled them both. Juliana instinctively stepped closer to Reggie, the world around her fading as she focused solely on him. It was then that their hands brushed—an accidental graze that sent a jolt of electricity racing up her arm, igniting her senses.

"Forgive me," he murmured, his voice low and steady, though she could see the flicker of surprise in his eyes. She held her breath, momentarily lost in the intimacy of the moment, feeling as if time itself had suspended.

"Not at all," she managed, her pulse quickening, betraying the calm she wished to project. The soft warmth of his skin lingered on hers, a fleeting connection that stirred something deep within her—a yearning mingled with trepidation.

"Shall we continue our exploration, then?" he asked, his tone shifting ever so slightly, as if he too felt the weight of their brief touch.

"Yes, let us," she replied, willing herself to move forward, even as uncertainty danced just beneath the surface. Together, they resumed their walk, laughter falling away, replaced by a shared silence that crackled with the promise of what lay unspoken.

As they continued their stroll, the air thick with the scent of blooming lilacs, Reggie's demeanor shifted. The lightness that had enveloped them dissipated like mist in the morning sun, leaving a dense fog of tension in its wake. He stopped short, turning to face her, his green eyes darkening with an emotion she could not quite decipher.

"Why did you not tell me about your engagement?" His voice was low, edged with hurt and frustration, cutting through the peaceful ambiance of the gardens. Juliana's heart sank at the weight of his question, the laughter that had danced between them now replaced by an oppressive silence.

"Reggie," she began, feeling the tremor in her own voice as she met his gaze. Words seemed to falter as uncertainty gripped her throat. She looked down at her hands, twisting the fabric of her gown, gathering her thoughts like scattered leaves before a tempest.

"Was I not worthy of that knowledge? Or is it merely a matter of convenience?" His tone held a sharpness that pierced through her defenses. She felt the sting of his words, each syllable a reminder of the distance that had grown between them.

"No, it is not that!" she exclaimed, her voice rising slightly, though she quickly tempered it. She took a breath, steadying herself against the torrent of emotions swirling within her. "I feared... I feared losing you, Reggie. You are my dearest friend. When I accepted Henri's proposal, I was consumed by uncertainty."

"Uncertainty?" he echoed, disbelief clouding his expression. "You chose him without ever confiding in me! Did you think I would dismiss your feelings as trivial?"

"That is not true!" she insisted, desperation creeping into her voice. "You must understand—I am expected to marry well; to fulfill my duty to my family." Her heart raced as she continued, "Henri is a man of considerable fortune and status. It seemed... sensible."

"Ah, sensible," he replied, his sarcasm palpable. "And what of your happiness, Juliana? Does that hold no merit in your decision?"

"Of course it does!" She pressed a hand to her chest, feeling the rapid beat beneath her fingertips. "But what good is happiness if it means sacrificing everything I have known? I could not bear to lose our friendship over something so uncertain."

"Then tell me, how can you be certain of this arrangement with him when you kept it hidden from me?" The hurt in his voice twisted like a knife, and she felt the ache of his disappointment as keenly as her own.

"Because I was terrified, Reggie!" The admission slipped out before she could stop it, raw and unfiltered. "Terrified that you would see me differently—that in unveiling my heart, I would find only rejection. I wanted to protect us both."

"Protect us?" His brows knitted together, disbelief mingling with pain. "Or protect yourself from facing the truth?"

"Perhaps both," she whispered, tears threatening to spill as vulnerability washed over her. "I thought... I thought I could navigate this alone. But now I see how foolish that was."

The garden around them faded into obscurity, the vibrant colors dulled by the weight of unvoiced feelings and unfulfilled desires. In the stillness, a fragile understanding flickered between them, yet the chasm of their unspoken truths loomed larger than ever, casting a long shadow over what lay ahead.

"Reggie, you must understand," Juliana implored, her voice rising with each frantic syllable. She paced before him on the narrow path, the manicured hedges towering like sentinels, indifferent to their turmoil. A gentle breeze rustled the leaves overhead, but it did nothing to quell the storm brewing between them.

"Understand?" Reggie's tone was sharp, his arms crossed tightly over his chest as if to shield himself from her words. "Is that truly what you believe? That I should simply accept your silence, your duplicity, while you prepare to bind yourself to another man?"

The accusation hung in the air, thick and suffocating. Juliana felt heat rise to her cheeks, a mix of indignation and despair churning within her. "I never meant to deceive you! This was not a choice made lightly. Henri… he offered security, a future when all I could see was uncertainty."

"Security?" He scoffed, the sound echoing against the distant hills. "What kind of security comes at the cost of honesty? You speak of futures, yet you deny me the truth of your present!"

"How could I tell you?" Her voice cracked under the weight of her emotion, and she halted, her hands trembling at her sides. "How could I risk losing what we have? You are my closest friend, Reggie. It is a bond forged through years of laughter and shared dreams. To lay bare my heart—" She paused, swallowed hard, fighting back the tide of tears threatening to spill forth. "To lay bare my heart would mean inviting the ruin of everything."

"Ruin?" he echoed, incredulity lacing his words. "You think keeping this hidden will protect us? It only deepens the divide between us! I cannot stand idly by while you prepare to marry a man who does not know you—who does not love you as I do!"

"Love?" The word fell from her lips like a whisper, frail and shivering with unacknowledged longing. "What do you know of love, Reggie? Perhaps this is merely a game for you, something to amuse yourself with while you gallivant through society."

"Amuse myself?" His voice rose further, frustration cracking through his carefully maintained composure. "You think I jest about my feelings? I care for you, Juliana! When I learned of your engagement, it felt as though the ground beneath me had given way. How do you expect me to remain silent?"

"Because the truth is painful!" she cried, tears finally spilling over, tracing delicate paths down her cheeks. "You do not understand the burden I carry. If you could only see how torn I am, perhaps you might find it in your heart to forgive me."

"Forgive you?" His tone softened, surprise flickering in his green eyes as he took a step closer, breaking the distance that had become a chasm between them. "This is not merely about forgiveness; it's about trust. Why could you not confide in me?"

"Because I feared your judgment," she confessed, her breath hitching as vulnerability enveloped her. "I feared you would view me as a fool, a woman willing to trade affection for security. But I need you to understand—I do not take this lightly. I am terrified of the unknown, of losing everything that has brought me solace."

"Juliana..." His voice dropped, carrying an earnestness that both soothed and unsettled her. "You have not lost me. Not yet. But you must let me in. You must allow me to bear witness to your struggles if we are to navigate this together."

"Together." The word lingered in the air, heavy with the weight of possibility. Juliana wiped at her tears, her heart aching with the desire for connection, the longing for him to see beyond her fear and into the depths of her soul. "Do you truly mean that?"

"Of course, I do." He stepped closer still, the warmth of his presence grounding her amidst the chaos of their emotions.

"But you must meet me halfway. We cannot move forward without honesty, Juliana."

"Then I shall try," she whispered, the tremor in her voice betraying her resolve. "I will try to be brave, for us both."

As the sun dipped lower in the sky, casting golden hues over the landscape, they stood there, their hearts entwined in the fragile promise of understanding, ready to face whatever came next.

Reggie's expression softened as he took a tentative step closer, the tension in his shoulders easing ever so slightly. He reached out, his fingers brushing against Juliana's cheek, where a tear had traced its path. The moisture was warm, and as he wiped it away, she felt an unfamiliar warmth bloom in her chest—a potent mixture of hope and fear.

"Juliana," he murmured, his voice low and steady, yet tinged with an urgency that made her heart race. His thumb lingered on her skin, a gentle caress that belied the storm of emotions swirling between them. In that moment, the world around them faded—the vibrant flowers and lush greenery blurred into insignificance. It was just the two of them, standing at the precipice of something profound.

"Why must you carry this burden alone?" His question hung in the air, weighted with unspoken confessions. Juliana searched his emerald eyes, desperate to decipher the tumult within him. Was there anger still simmering beneath the surface? Or was it merely the remnants of their earlier confrontation, now replaced by concern?

"Because I do not wish to drag you into my turmoil," she replied, her voice barely above a whisper. Her own tears threatened to spill anew, but she fought to contain them, unwilling to show any further vulnerability. Yet here they were—entwined in a silence charged with everything left unsaid, the air thick with a yearning that both terrified and exhilarated her.

They stood frozen, each heartbeat echoing louder than the last. The sun began its descent, casting long shadows across the manicured lawn, and the soft rustle of leaves whispered secrets of love and loss. Their gazes locked, a battle of longing and uncertainty waged silently between them.

"Do you see me, Reggie?" she finally asked, her breath catching in her throat. "Truly see me?"

"More than you know." His words unfurled like silk, smooth and tender, yet laden with the weight of all they had shared. With every lingering second, the distance between them shrank, and she felt the gravity of their connection pull her forward.

"Then understand," she pressed, the fire of determination igniting within her. "I am afraid—afraid of losing your friendship, of stepping beyond the boundaries we've set for ourselves."

"Boundaries," he echoed, a hint of bitterness lacing his tone. "What if those very boundaries are what keep us from happiness?"

The question hung in the air, heavy and unyielding. Juliana's pulse quickened, a mix of dread and exhilaration coursing through her veins. She wanted to reach out, to bridge the gap between them, but the uncertainty of what lay ahead held her captive.

"Reggie..." she started, but the words faltered on her lips, trapped by the weight of their history and the potential of their future.

"Let us not remain shackled by what others expect of us," he urged, his gaze intense and unwavering. "We have the power to forge our own path. Together."

Together. The word resonated deep within her, a promise wrapped in possibility. But could they truly defy the conventions that governed their lives? The gravity of the choice loomed large, and still they remained, suspended in a moment that felt eternal.

As the last rays of sunlight dipped below the horizon, casting a soft twilight glow over them, Juliana felt the tremors of change ripple through the air. She could not deny the intensity of her feelings for Reggie, nor the way his presence ignited a fire within her that demanded to be acknowledged.

"Together," she finally whispered, the resolve settling in her heart, fragile yet resolute. Their hands brushed once more, lingering in a connection that spoke volumes, and as the night enveloped them, the uncharted territory of their emotions beckoned like the stars beginning to twinkle overhead.

The silence stretched between them, heavy with unspoken truths, until Reggie finally drew a breath that seemed to echo in the stillness of the fading light. He stepped closer, grounding himself in the moment, and let out a heavy sigh that spoke of resignation yet held a flicker of determination.

"Juliana," he began, his voice steady but low, "we must find a way through this... labyrinth of emotions." His green eyes searched hers, filled with a mix of vulnerability and resolve. "We cannot allow our choices to bind us like shackles. We owe it to ourselves to navigate these turbulent waters."

Juliana's heart raced, her spirit caught between the two opposing forces of hope and fear. She could scarcely breathe as she absorbed the weight of his words. "You mean... face it together?" she asked, her voice barely above a whisper, though the tremor betrayed the storm brewing within her.

"Yes," he affirmed, taking another step forward, their proximity igniting a tension that crackled like the last sparks of a dying flame. "Together. But we must be honest—truly honest—with one another."

It was an invitation wrapped in a challenge, and she felt her pulse quicken. The thought of sharing her innermost fears, her doubts about Henri de Beaumont's proposal, sent a shiver of trepidation coursing through her. Yet, nestled within that trepidation was something else, a burgeoning sense of courage that had lain dormant for far too long.

"Reggie, I—" she hesitated, gathering the strength to bare her soul. "I am terrified of losing what we have. This friendship means everything to me. What if my engagement changes it all?"

"Then let us redefine what it can be," he interjected, urgency threading through his tone. "We can create something new, something that transcends the constraints of society's expectations. But it begins with honesty."

A warmth spread through her at his words, igniting a flicker of hope deep within her chest. "You promise that we will not lose each other?" Juliana's voice trembled as she sought reassurance, desperate for his affirmation.

"Absolutely," he replied, reaching for her hand once more. His touch was gentle, a tether that steadied her racing heart. "No matter what lies ahead, I refuse to let go of you."

With the moonlight beginning to cast its ethereal glow around them, illuminating the path before them, a fragile lifeline formed—one woven from their shared commitment to face the trials that loomed on the horizon.

Seven

Reggie navigated the throng of elegantly dressed nobility, the hum of whispered conversations and the delicate clinking of crystal permeating the grand ballroom. Lady Meredith moved through the crowd towards him, her golden hair catching the soft candlelight with each poised step she took. As she neared, Reggie noted the slight furrow that marred her usually serene brow—a subtle testament to the disquiet brewing within her.

"Reginald," she began, her voice a gentle murmur amid the orchestral swell, "I must implore you for candor on a matter most troubling." Her gaze locked onto his, azure eyes probing for the merest hint of evasion. "Your behavior of late has been...most perplexing. Tell me, have your intentions towards our engagement wavered?"

Reggie felt the weight of her scrutiny like a physical force. He had not anticipated such directness from Meredith; it was unlike her to confront so openly. With practiced ease, he conjured a smile, one corner of his mouth lifting in an attempt to disarm her concerns.

"Dearest Meredith," he replied, his tone light, though a flutter of unease stirred within him. "Surely you jest to question my steadfastness. Our union remains as unshaken as ever." He raised his hand, dismissing the very notion of doubt with a casual flick of his wrist.

"Yet, even the firmest of foundations may reveal cracks upon closer inspection," she countered, undeterred by his charm. Her words were coated with an undeniable strain, betraying the gravity of her apprehensions.

"Rest assured, there exists no fissure between us," Reggie asserted, though the affirmation rang hollow even to his own ears. "My commitment to you, and to the prosperous future awaiting us, is as resolute as the day our betrothal was announced."

Lady Meredith regarded him a moment longer, the dance of emotions across her features suggesting an internal debate.

"Reginald," Meredith's voice held an edge of entreaty, her dainty hand reaching out to pause his retreat. "Pray, do not don a mask with me. Speak plainly." The candlelight flickered across the high cheekbones that lent her face such refined elegance, casting shadows that seemed to deepen the urgency in her striking blue eyes.

Reggie faltered, the rehearsed assurances dying on his lips. Her plea resonated with a sincerity that shook the composure he so meticulously maintained. He could no longer ignore the silent plea for transparency in her gaze, nor the subtle quiver that betrayed her usual serenity.

"Your apprehension...it is not without merit," he confessed, his voice a mere whisper amongst the symphony of the ballroom. His own admission startled him, the truth springing forth like a coiled serpent suddenly released.

Meredith's brow creased, her poise momentarily slipping at his unexpected candor. "You speak in riddles, my lord. If there is aught amiss, I must insist you reveal it."

With a heavy heart, Reggie watched the hope in her eyes wane under the gravity of his hesitation. A gentleman would shield her from such distress, but honor bade him unburden his soul. "Juliana," he began, the name itself a torment, "her engagement to another has..." His words trailed off as he wrestled with the tempest within.

"Has what, Reginald?" she pressed, the desperation now clear in her tone. Her hand, once so sure upon his sleeve, trembled with a vulnerability he had not seen before.

"Haunted me," he admitted, the raw honesty of his declaration hanging between them like a specter. The weight of his gaze shifted from Meredith's expectant face to the gilded floor, where the intricate patterns provided no solace from the storm of consequences he had unleashed.

"Haunted you," Meredith echoed, her voice hollow as she absorbed the implications of his turmoil. "And yet we are to be wed."

"Indeed," he replied, the word tasting of ashes. In his heart, he knew the folly of his position, caught between duty and desire. But the truth remained, laid bare before her like a challenge neither of them was prepared to accept.

"Consider, Reginald," she continued, her composure regained through sheer force of will, "the impact of your...preoccupations...on our families, on our future."

He could only nod, aware that the path he tread was fraught with peril. The revelation had set them adrift in uncertain waters, and how they navigated the tides of society's expectations would determine much more than their own fates.

* * *

JULIANA FLOATED on the edges of the ballroom, her sparkling blue eyes adrift in a sea of twirling figures and vibrant gowns. Each measured step she took was a silent testament to her poise, yet beneath the veneer of calm, her pulse quickened with the thrill of the clandestine. In the labyrinth of high society's dance, she sought just one face—a beacon that might anchor her restless spirit.

She wove through clusters of laughter and idle gossip, each word falling upon her ears as if from a distance. A fervent quest drove her forward, for amidst the throng, it was Messingham alone who could stir the embers of yearning within her breast. His absence was a void no gallantry or flattery from other suitors could fill; his presence, the only remedy to the disquiet that plagued her heart.

Across the room, amidst the rustle of silk and the delicate clink of crystal, Reggie stood immobilized by the revelation that had escaped his lips moments prior. The truth of his sentiments lay bare, a scandalous undercurrent beneath the decorum of the evening. As he sought to regain his composure, the sight of Juliana's auburn locks catching the candlelight offered him little respite.

His resolve crystallized in an instant. With the stealth of a predator and the grace of nobility, Reggie threaded his way through the assembly. The air of conviviality around him paled in contrast to the singular focus that propelled him towards Juliana. His tall frame maneuvered with a swiftness belying the cacophony of emotions that clamored within him.

Juliana paused, her breath hitching ever so slightly as a familiar energy seemed to beckon her. She continued her circuitous path, unaware that her silent admirer now navigated the ballroom with deliberate intent. In the waltz of glances and gestures, she remained oblivious to the determined approach of the man whose very thoughts could command her attention without utterance.

As Reggie neared, the space between them dwindled, charged with unsaid truths and unexplored possibilities. The pull of their shared past—a tapestry woven from years of discreet glances and half-whispered confidences—was a force more compelling than the music that filled the room.

He was but steps away when she turned, her gaze alighting upon another, causing his heart to falter for the briefest of moments. It was then, in that pause betwixt heartbeats, that the future loomed before them both, a precipice from which there was no retreating. With a breath drawn deep into his lungs, Reggie pressed on, his determination unwavering as he readied himself to close the distance, to breach the chasm of propriety, and to claim the moment that fate had conspired to present.

Juliana's senses sharpened as the hum of conversation and the lilting strains of a string quartet faded into the background. A subtle shift in the air alerted her to Reggie's proximity before she even saw him. Her spine stiffened, an electric current of awareness tingling down her back. She turned slowly, the silk of her gown whispering against the polished floor, her eyes lifting to meet his.

Their gazes locked, and for a moment, the world ceased its relentless spin. Juliana's breath lodged in her throat, her pulse hammering with the intensity of their silent communion. In Reggie's eyes, a tempest swirled—a storm of longing and unspoken promises that resonated within her own heart. The space between them charged with an energy that seemed to defy the decorum of their surroundings.

Reggie's approach was inexorable, his steps measured but resolute as he closed the distance between them. His very presence commanded her attention, a beacon amidst the sea of gilded guests and swirling dancers. As he drew near, Juliana felt the weight of expectation, the gravity of years of hidden yearning pulling them closer, an invisible thread woven through the fabric of their shared history.

The moment he reached her, Reggie acted with a decisiveness that betrayed the roiling emotions beneath his composed exterior. His hand extended, fingers wrapping around Juliana's arm with a touch that was both assertive and tender. The contact sent a jolt through her, a silent acknowledgment of all they dared not speak aloud.

"Come with me," he murmured, his voice low and urgent, the words for her ears alone.

Without waiting for an answer, he guided her away from the throng of oblivious revelers, toward the shadowed edge of the ballroom. Juliana moved with him, her mind a whirlwind of apprehension and anticipation, instinctively trusting him to lead her from the glaring lights and prying eyes.

They passed through tall French doors left ajar, the cool night air a welcome reprieve from the stifling warmth of the crowded room. The manicured gardens, bathed in moonlight, offered a sanctuary of privacy where the strictures of society could not reach. Reggie did not slow until they were ensconced among the tall trees and fragrant blooms, far removed from the watchful gaze of their peers.

Juliana's pulse thrummed in her ears as she allowed Reggie to guide her deeper into the solitude of the garden, her silk slippers whispering secrets against the gravel path. Each step was a silent conversation between doubt and desire, a delicate dance of propriety and passion that left her breathless with its intensity.

"Juliana," Reggie began, his voice a low rumble of emotion that resonated through the quiet night, "I can no longer feign indifference or hide behind the façade of friendship we've so carefully maintained."

In the shadows cast by flickering lanterns, his face was a study of earnest anguish. Juliana felt the gravity of his confession before words even graced his lips, the air around them thick with unspoken truths.

"Ever since we were children, I have found myself drawn to you, inexplicably tethered by a force greater than mere fondness. And now, with every suitor that parades before you, my heart constricts with a jealousy I cannot quell." His green eyes searched hers, seeking solace for a torment she had glimpsed but never fully understood until this moment.

"Reggie, please...we mustn't," Juliana whispered, her resolve waning under the weight of his gaze, even as her own heart clamored in agreement.

"Mustn't we?" he countered, stepping closer, the space between them charged with the energy of forbidden yearnings. "Tell me, dearest Juliana, does your heart not race as mine does? Does the prospect of a lifetime without the other not fill you with dread so profound it steals your very breath?"

Her chest heaved, a silent testament to the confession that lingered on the tip of her tongue—a declaration that could shatter the fragile structure of their societal standing.

"Reggie," she breathed, the name a caress that spoke volumes of the years of camaraderie, of glances laden with meaning, of laughter, shared in golden-lit drawing rooms—of everything unsaid that now hung suspended in the cool night air.

"Juliana," he said, his voice laced with a desperation that mirrored the pounding of her heart, "to see you joined to another would be my undoing. The thought alone is..." He faltered, the usual eloquence abandoned in favor of raw honesty.

A silence enveloped them, filled only by the distant strains of music from the ballroom and the crescendo of their shared heartbeat. In that moment, Juliana knew the precarious edge upon which they stood—a precipice overlooking either utter ruin or sublime fulfillment.

"Messingham, what are we to do?" Her voice was a soft echo of the turmoil that roiled within, a plea for guidance in navigating the treacherous waters of their affections.

"Juliana, my dear, I am as adrift as you," Reggie confessed, his usually confident demeanor surrendering to the vulnerability of a man conquered by love. "But if there is any chance for us, any possibility that we might claim a future together, I will risk it all—for what is a life without you, but a hollow existence?"

The moonlight cast a silvery glow upon the clandestine rendezvous, illuminating Juliana's face as it was lit with a constellation of emotions. Her blue eyes, wide and luminous in the shadowed alcove of the garden, never left Reggie's gaze. With a trembling hand, she reached out to him, her fingers brushing against the rough stubble on his cheek. In that touch, an entire sonnet of longing was written, more poignant than any words they might have dared to speak.

"Reginald," she whispered, her voice barely audible above the rustle of leaves in the gentle night breeze.

"Juliana," he breathed back, his own voice thick with emotion.

That single utterance was a key turning in a lock, releasing years of restrained passion. Their lips met then, fiercely and without reservation as if all the pent-up yearning of their souls had found its expression in this one act. The kiss deepened, fervent and consuming, a conflagration that threatened to lay bare every pretense and propriety they had ever known.

Unbeknownst to them, another soul traversed the same secluded path, drawn by the lure of the same moonlit solitude. Lady Meredith St. Clair, her elegant figure garbed in the finest silk, moved with a grace born of countless balls and soirees. Yet tonight, her usual poise faltered as the sight before her drew a sharp, pained breath from her chest.

Her footsteps halted, resonating like a knell of doom upon the gravel path, as she beheld the man to whom she had given her guarded heart entwined with another. Her eyes, twin pools of azure, widened not merely in surprise but in the sting of betrayal—the kind of hurt that cuts deeper than the sharpest blade.

For a moment frozen in time, Meredith's gaze lingered on the pair, her visage a tableau of shock and sorrow. Then, as though rousing from a spell, she turned away, her departure silent save for the soft whisper of her skirts against the foliage. Her retreat was dignified but hasty, her figure soon swallowed by the shadows as she made her way back to the ballroom, leaving behind only the echo of her heartbreak amidst the roses and the ivy.

Reggie and Juliana remained locked in their embrace, unaware that the future they had just dared to dream might have crumbled before it could even begin to take shape.

Reggie's heart raced as the space between him and Juliana shrank to nothing, their breaths mingling in the cool night air. The fervor of their kiss waned, leaving a silence thick with unvoiced promises and uncharted dreams. They parted, their gazes locked in a silent exchange that spoke volumes more than words ever could. In the luminescence of the moonlight, sorrow and desire etched deep into their features, reflecting a turmoil only lovers could know.

"Reggie," Juliana whispered, her voice a ghostly echo among the rustling leaves. "You must go to Meredith. She deserves the truth, however grievous it may be."

He searched her eyes, finding there an abyss of resignation and fortitude. Her fingers, so delicate against his jaw just moments ago, now fell to her side, relinquishing their tender hold. Reggie felt the weight of his choices like chains upon his soul. With a nod, he acknowledged the gravity of the path ahead.

"Juliana," he murmured, struggling to cloak his anguish with a veneer of resolve. "I shall speak with her, though I fear my words will scarce mend what has been rent asunder this eve."

Turning from Juliana, Reggie's steps were hesitant as if each footfall carried the burden of their stolen love. His gaze lingered on her for a mere heartbeat longer before he forced himself to stride back toward the stately manor, where candlelight danced through the windows, mocking the darkness that now enveloped his heart. The whispers of the night seemed to carry both hope and despair, entwined like the lives they had just risked with a single, illicit kiss.

Reggie's silhouette diminished into the shadowy embrace of the grand estate, and Juliana stood motionless amidst the fragrant blossoms, her breath a delicate vapor in the crisp night air. The echo of his steps faded, leaving her ensnared in a silence that seemed to reverberate with the thudding of her own heart. She watched, the hope within her warring with the despair that sought to claim dominion over her senses.

A shiver coursed through her, not from the evening's chill but from the knowledge of the precipice upon which they now teetered. With a slow exhale that bespoke an attempt at composure, Juliana's gaze drifted from the path Reggie had taken to the heavens above. Stars, indifferent in their celestial ballet, offered no counsel to the turmoil that churned beneath them.

Drawing her shawl tighter around her shoulders, the fabric whispered across her skin like the murmur of scandal that would soon ensue should their indiscretion be laid bare. Juliana knew the weight of expectation that bore down upon a woman of her standing. Yet, as she considered the labyrinthine journey ahead, it was not the societal consequence that tightened its grip upon her soul—it was the ache of longing for what could never be.

Eight

As Reggie rounded the corner of the hedged path, his thoughts still dancing with the thrill of Juliana's stolen kiss, he collided sharply with a figure that seemed to materialize from the very shadows.

"Ah, Your Grace," said Mr. Percival Worthington, adjusting his cravat with an air of insouciance. The moonlight glinted off his polished shoes as he stepped back, a thin smile tugging at the corners of his lips. "What a fortuitous meeting." His voice, smooth and deliberate, carried an undertone of something darker.

Reggie straightened, his heart thrumming in his chest. He met Worthington's gaze, those piercing eyes glinting with knowing malice that sent unease skittering across his skin. "Mr. Worthington," he replied, forcing a cordiality into his tone that felt like biting into a sour apple. "What brings you here?"

"Merely enjoying the gardens, my lord," Worthington replied, his expression shifting to one of feigned concern. "But I must confess, I chanced upon quite the spectacle earlier—a rather intimate encounter between yourself and Lady Langdon." The words slithered off his tongue, each syllable calculated to wound.

A chill settled in the pit of Reggie's stomach. "You misinterpret—" he began, but Worthington raised a hand, silencing him with a gesture so dismissive it stung.

"Forgive me, but I assure you, no interpretation is necessary. A gentleman such as myself appreciates the nuances of... affection." His smile widened, yet there was no warmth behind it. "I simply wonder how your family would fare should such indiscretions come to light. The Haine name carries weight in society, does it not?"

Reggie clenched his jaw, the implications of Worthington's insinuations pressing heavily on his shoulders. "I trust my reputation remains intact by my own actions, Mr. Worthington."

"Ah, but reputations are fragile things, my lord," Worthington purred, leaning closer, his breath a whisper of danger. "And a single breath of scandal can shatter even the most esteemed lineage." He straightened, restoring the distance between them, though the threat lingered like smoke in the air. "Should you find yourself in need of protection for your esteemed family, rest assured I am well-acquainted with the intricacies of social maneuvering. One might say I have a talent for... persuasion." The malicious glint in his eye was unmistakable, a predator reveling in its prey's vulnerability.

Reggie met his gaze with steely resolve, suppressing the instinctual flare of anger that threatened to erupt. "Be careful, Mr. Worthington," Reggie warned, his voice low but firm. "Threatening my family is a dangerous endeavor."

"Is it a threat, my lord? Or merely a friendly reminder?" Worthington chuckled softly, the sound devoid of genuine mirth. "After all, we wouldn't want to see any unfortunate tales spread through the drawing rooms of London, now would we?"

With that, he turned on his heel, leaving Reggie standing in the garden's embrace, a sense of foreboding settling around him like a shroud. The exhilaration of that secret kiss faded into cold dread, and with it came the realization that their love might soon be ensnared in a web of scandal.

JULIANA KNELT among the blooming roses, their vibrant petals a stark contrast to the turmoil brewing within her heart. She had sought solace in the garden, the fragrant air and rustling leaves momentarily distracting her from the world beyond. Yet, tranquility fled as she sensed a presence drawing nearer.

"Lady Juliana," a smooth voice cut through the air, dripping with honeyed malice.

She looked up, her breath catching at the sight of Mr. Percival Worthington, his tall frame casting an imposing shadow over her dainty figure. His piercing gaze locked onto hers, revealing a calculated amusement that sent a chill down her spine.

"Mr. Worthington," she replied, attempting to maintain her composure. "What brings you here?"

"Ah, but I believe you know precisely why I'm here." He took a step closer, his voice lowering to a conspiratorial whisper. "I witnessed quite an intriguing moment between you and Messingham just moments ago—a kiss so sweet it could tempt even the most virtuous."

The color drained from Juliana's cheeks, panic rising like bile in her throat. "You—" She faltered, struggling for words. "You have no right to speak of such things."

"On the contrary." His smile widened, revealing the predator beneath the polished exterior. "It is precisely my right, especially when such indiscretions threaten one's standing in society. A kiss shared in secret can easily transform into scandal, don't you think? The Haine family would hardly appreciate the fallout of your... impetuousness."

Her mind raced, the implications of his threat crashing over her like a sudden storm. Reggie's reputation, his esteemed family—her heart twisted at the thought of them tarnished by her actions. "What do you want from me?" she asked, her voice trembling despite her best efforts to sound resolute.

"Compliance is all I seek, dear lady." He leaned in further, his breath cool against her skin. "You will ensure that our little rendezvous remains under wraps. In return, I shall keep this charming episode of yours a secret. However, should you choose to defy me, I cannot guarantee the same discretion."

Juliana's thoughts spiraled. The idea of sacrificing her happiness to shield Reggie felt unbearably heavy. Could she bear the weight of such a decision? Each potential consequence ricocheted in her mind, a cacophony of fear and dread. The laughter of the ton echoed ominously in her ears, painting vivid images of whispers and pointed fingers, of a life lived under the shadow of disgrace.

"Should you decide otherwise," he continued, his voice slicing through her reverie, "the repercussions will not only affect you but extend far beyond. A mere gossip could ruin everything for both families. Are you willing to risk that?"

A knot of despair tightened in her chest. She was trapped between her love and loyalty to Reggie and the sinister manipulations of Worthington. Each heartbeat pulsed with the reality of her choices. If she agreed, she would effectively relinquish her dreams, her future intertwined with a man she loved, all for the sake of protecting him.

"Think well on it, Lady Juliana," Worthington purred, straightening up and tipping his hat with mock politeness. "I shall expect your answer soon. After all, time waits for no one, least of all in matters of reputation."

As he turned and strode away, leaving her alone amidst the roses, Juliana felt the world closing in around her. The sun dipped lower in the sky, shadows lengthening across the manicured lawn, and with each passing moment, the weight of her dilemma pressed heavily upon her heart. Would she sacrifice her own happiness to shield the man she adored? The answer lay just beyond reach, shrouded in uncertainty and fear.

* * *

REGGIE ROUNDED the corner of the hedged pathway, his heart pounding against his ribs like a war drum. The sun dipped lower in the sky, casting a golden hue over the garden, but he hardly noticed its beauty; his mind was consumed with thoughts of Juliana. He had to find her—had to ensure she was safe from Worthington's insidious machinations.

As he approached the rose arbor, he caught sight of her silhouette framed by the delicate blooms, her auburn hair catching the last rays of the day. But even from afar, he sensed an unsettling stillness that sent a chill racing up his spine. "Juliana!" he called out, urgency threading through his voice as he quickened his pace.

She turned, her expression shifting from surprise to something more guarded, and Reggie felt a knot tighten in his stomach. The moment he reached her side, he noted the faint tremor in her hands, the way her eyes darted away from his gaze. "What did he say to you?"

"Reggie, I—" she began, but he couldn't bear to hear her finish. The knowledge of Worthington's threats loomed large, a specter hanging over them both.

"That man is dangerous," he said, anger boiling beneath his calm facade. "He must not have said anything that would jeopardize your standing, or ours." Each word dripped with tension, a desperate plea for reassurance.

"His words were... pointed," she admitted, lowering her gaze to the ground. "It seems he witnessed our kiss."

Reggie's breath caught in his throat, fury igniting within him. "He dares to use our affection against us? To threaten you?" The very thought of Worthington's twisted intentions made his blood boil. A helpless rage coursed through him; how could someone manipulate love so cruelly?

"Reggie, please," she urged softly, stepping closer, though the distance between them felt vast. "We are not safe. His threats—they're not idle. If he exposes what happened, it will ruin everything."

"Let him try!" Reggie snapped, frustration bubbling over. "I will not allow him to dictate our lives, nor shall I stand idly by while he threatens you!"

"Your name, your family—" she protested, her voice trembling, but he could see the conflict swirling in her blue eyes. She was fighting a battle within herself, torn between their love and the looming repercussions of defiance.

"Do you truly believe I care for reputation over my feelings for you?" he challenged, his voice dropping to an intense whisper. "I will fight for us!"

"Fighting may only make things worse," she replied, her tone heavy with sorrow. "If I do not comply with him, it is not just my happiness at stake. Think of your family, Reggie. I cannot bear to be the cause of your disgrace."

Silence hung thick in the air, the weight of unspoken truths pressing down on them. While Reggie's heart rebelled against such notions, he could sense the fear driving her resolve. They were trapped, each caught in the web of Worthington's schemes, and the walls closed tighter around them with every passing moment.

"Juliana, we can find a way…" he murmured, desperation creeping into his voice.

"Can we?" she asked, her brow furrowed in anguish. "Every option leads back to him. I cannot let this destroy you. It would break me to know my choices brought harm to those I love."

Reggie stepped back, the enormity of their predicament crashing down upon him. He could feel the gulf widening between them, a chasm carved by fate and the cunning of a man who thrived on manipulation. As she looked away, he saw a flicker of determination in her posture—a resolve that frightened him.

"Perhaps distancing ourselves is the only solution," she whispered, her voice barely audible, yet the words struck him like a physical blow.

"Juliana, no!" he exclaimed, grasping her hands in a plea to anchor her to him. "You cannot mean that! We can face this together."

The tears glimmering in her eyes betrayed the turmoil within her, even as she steeled herself against him. "Together may lead us to destruction," she murmured, pulling her hands from his grasp. "Sometimes it is best to protect those we love by setting them free."

As she stepped back, the space between them widened, and Reggie's heart sank under the weight of despair. The garden, once a sanctuary of their shared dreams, now felt like a prison forged by Worthington's nefarious designs. With each passing moment, it became painfully clear: they were both on the precipice of sacrifice, teetering between love and the bitter reality of their situation.

* * *

ACROSS THE ESTATE, Lady Meredith paced along the corridor of the grand drawing room, her thoughts tangled between concern and bewilderment. She spotted Mr. Worthington lingering near the window, his silhouette sharp against the soft glow of the late afternoon light. His presence stirred unease in her heart, though she could not decipher why.

"Lady Meredith," he began, turning slowly to face her, a glimmer of false sympathy brightening his piercing gaze. "I trust you are well in these tumultuous times?" He approached her with an elegance that belied the malice lurking behind his charming facade.

"Quite well, thank you, Mr. Worthington," she replied cautiously, sensing the tension in the air thickening as he drew nearer. "But I am troubled by recent events…"

"Ah, yes. Such distressing matters can weigh heavily, indeed." He leaned closer, lowering his voice to a conspiratorial whisper. "It must be dreadful to feel one's reputation hanging by a mere thread. I shudder to think how the ton would react to indiscretions."

The way he spoke, smooth and calculated, sent a shiver down Lady Meredith's spine. She forced herself to maintain eye contact, unwilling to show him any sign of her discomfort.

"Indiscretions?" she echoed, feigning ignorance, though her instincts screamed otherwise.

"Indeed. A fleeting moment can unravel the finest of reputations," he said, his voice dripping with false concern. "But fear not, my lady. I have always found myself inclined to assist those in need." The way he framed his words felt like a noose tightening around her neck.

"Your kindness is noted, Mr. Worthington," she replied, her heart racing with confusion. Despite the polished exterior, something was amiss. "However, I assure you, I require no assistance."

"Are you certain?" he pressed, the corners of his mouth curling into a smile that did not reach his eyes. "For I would hate to see anything untoward happen to someone as exquisite as yourself."

Lady Meredith felt her pulse quicken, alarm bells ringing in her mind. She stepped back imperceptibly, trying to gauge his intentions. There was something predatory in his demeanor, a darkness lurking just beneath his polished surface. Each word dripped with a syrupy sweetness that made her skin crawl.

"Mr. Worthington, I appreciate your concern, but I assure you, my family stands firm against any slander." She spoke carefully, her voice steady despite her racing thoughts.

"Then perhaps you might consider allowing me to keep a watchful eye," he suggested, his tone now edged with an unsettling insistence. "After all, a lady of your standing deserves protection—especially from unscrupulous gentlemen who might take advantage of vulnerability."

"Yes, but at what cost?" she questioned softly, her instincts flaring as she sensed the true nature of his proposal. Beneath his veneer of gallantry lay the unmistakable stench of manipulation.

"Nothing more than what is owed to you, dear lady," he replied, his voice silkily persuasive. "Merely a gesture of goodwill for someone destined to shine brightly in society."

Lady Meredith swallowed hard, the weight of his insinuation pressing down upon her. As he lingered before her, the threads of his intentions wove themselves into a tapestry of dread. Something within her urged caution, a primal instinct warning her to tread carefully.

"Be wary, Mr. Worthington," she warned, her voice strong despite her growing apprehension. "For I am not easily swayed by empty promises."

"Of course," he replied smoothly, although the flash of irritation in his eyes betrayed him. "But remember, sometimes the most innocent of gestures can carry the greatest burden."

As their conversation continued, Lady Meredith's unease deepened. She felt ensnared in a game far beyond her comprehension, and the stakes were higher than she ever imagined. With every word exchanged, the grip of foreboding tightened around her heart, and her instincts screamed for her to escape the silken trap he had spun.

JULIANA TURNED AWAY FROM REGGIE, her heart pounding as if it sought to break free from the constraints of her determination. Each step she took felt like a betrayal, the manicured grass beneath her feet whispering secrets of their shared past, memories that now stung like nettles upon her skin. The garden, once a sanctuary, transformed into a prison where every bloom echoed the laughter they had shared.

"Why must it come to this?" she thought, pushing aside the ache that threatened to swallow her whole. "I cannot allow him to harm you, Reggie. This is my burden to bear." The weight of her resolve pressed against her chest, an unbearable heaviness that left no room for doubt.

"Enough," she urged herself, the echo of his voice still ringing in her ears—a melody tinged with desperation and longing. She could almost feel his green eyes upon her, questioning, pleading. "You are doing this for him. You must think of your family, of his family." Yet, the thought only deepened her sorrow. A sacrifice was never truly noble when it meant losing the very thing she cherished most.

"Farewell," she whispered to the wind, hoping the words would carry back to him, though she knew they would not suffice. Their love had always felt like a fragile bubble, buoyant yet precarious, and now it threatened to burst under the strain of Mr. Worthington's malicious grip.

As she neared the edge of the garden, her gaze flickered back to where he stood—tall, resolute, yet so utterly lost. He appeared like a statue of anguish, his features carved from stone, etched with disbelief at the abrupt ending of something so beautiful. Her breath caught in her throat; the sight of him sent a jolt through her heart, igniting a spark of rebellion against her own decision.

"Could I not simply tell him the truth? That I love him? That I will always love him?" The thought flitted through her mind like a desperate bird seeking escape. But just as quickly, the cold reality settled in. To speak those words would invite ruin —not only for herself but for him, too.

"Mr. Worthington would delight in such folly. This must be done."

With each step, the distance between them felt insurmountable. And yet, she pressed on, forcing herself to walk away, her fingers brushing against the soft fabric of her gown as if it tethered her to the moment, to him. "What am I sacrificing?" she pondered, the question reverberating through her thoughts. "Is it love, or merely the illusion of happiness?"

"Keep moving," she commanded inwardly, her pulse quickening, driven by the need to reach the safety of the estate. But her heart lingered, shackled to the man who might forever remain a distant dream.

"How cruel fate can be," she mused bitterly, glancing over her shoulder one last time. She saw him there, silhouetted by the fading light, an image that would haunt her long after she departed. "To love yet know it may never blossom."

With a final shuddering breath, Juliana turned away, her face a mask of determination, her steps laden with the profound weight of sacrifice. As she walked into the twilight, the shadows danced around her, mirroring the turmoil that churned within. Love, she realized, was a battlefield—one where victory came at a cost steeped in heartache.

"Perhaps someday, in another life," she dared to dream, though the thought felt like sand slipping through her fingers. "But for now, I must protect him." And with that thought, she stepped into the encroaching darkness, leaving behind the promise of what could have been, knowing that their love might never be realized.

Nine

The sun dipped low on the horizon, casting elongated shadows across the manicured lawns of Langdon House. Lady Juliana Langdon paced within the confines of her chamber, her fingers nervously twisting a delicate lace handkerchief. Each step echoed her resolve and doubt—a tumultuous dance between loyalty and duty.

"How could I abandon them?" she whispered to herself, glancing out the window toward the distant silhouette of the Messingham estate. The sight of it stirred a pang in her chest, a reminder of laughter shared over tea and the warmth of familial bonds. Yet, the specter of Mr. Percival Worthington loomed larger with each passing day, his charming demeanor concealing a depth of ambition that unsettled her.

"To protect them is my burden," she murmured, recalling the steely glint in Worthington's eyes during their last encounter —a glance that had sent shivers down her spine. It was not mere attraction but something darker, an insidious hunger for power that threatened to devour all she held dear. Her heart clenched; the thought of Reggie and his family ensnared in such a web made her stomach churn.

With renewed determination, she pressed a palm against the cool glass of the window, as if seeking clarity through its transparency. "I must uncover his intentions." The plan crystallized within her mind, sharp and resolute. Disguised as casual observation, she would weave herself into the very fabric of society, threading through gatherings where Worthington might reveal himself, his true nature lurking beneath layers of charm.

"Perhaps the next soirée at Lady Fletcher's will serve as my stage," she mused, a hint of steel creeping into her voice. The opulent ballroom—a veritable hive of gossip and intrigue—would be the perfect locale for her inquiries. She envisioned herself mingling among the elite, a subtle observer amidst the swirling gowns and glittering cravats, keenly attuned to Worthington's interactions.

"Conversations can expose secrets," she reminded herself, picturing the delicate art of social navigation. With every comment and laugh, she would root out the truths hidden in whispered exchanges, the silent betrayals masked by polite smiles.

The weight of her responsibilities pressed heavily upon her shoulders, yet with each heartbeat, her purpose solidified. To shield the Haine family from Worthington's machinations, she would become the unseen sentinel, gathering evidence like pearls from the depths of a treacherous sea.

"Let him think me naïve," Juliana resolved, her blue eyes narrowing with fierce resolve. "Underestimating me shall be his greatest error." The stakes were high, and her heart raced at the thought of the dangers ahead, but she welcomed the challenge. For love and loyalty, she would embrace her role as both protector and investigator, ready to confront whatever darkness lay ahead in her pursuit of truth.

* * *

THE SOIRÉE at Lady Fletcher's unfolded like a grand tapestry, each thread woven with laughter and whispered secrets. Lady Juliana Langdon swept into the ballroom, her auburn hair gleaming under the crystal chandeliers as she scanned the crowd with keen blue eyes. The scent of roses and polished wood enveloped her, a heady perfume that masked the tension gathering in her chest.

"Lady Juliana! You must join us!" called out Lady Fitzwilliam, her voice lilting over the din of chatter. Juliana offered a polite smile, but her heart raced for another reason entirely.

"Perhaps later, my dear," she replied, her words carefully measured as she turned her attention to a cluster of gentlemen near the refreshment table. Among them stood Mr. Percival Worthington, his dapper figure commanding attention. He was engaged in conversation, his smooth voice weaving through the air like silk, drawing listeners nearer with every charming inflection.

Juliana took a step back, allowing the ebb and flow of the social tide to carry her closer. As she grasped a glass of lemonade—refreshing yet decidedly innocuous—she listened attentively, pretending to admire the delicate pastries arranged on a silver platter.

"Did you hear? Worthington is courting Lady Charlotte Durmontt," one gentleman remarked, a hint of incredulity in his tone. "Such a match! But can anyone truly trust him?"

"Trust is a fickle companion, indeed," another chimed in, leaning closer. "There are whispers of dealings that would make even the most daring blush."

With each word, a flicker of hope ignited within Juliana. This was it—the chink in Worthington's polished armor. She leaned in slightly, feigning interest in the pastry selection while straining to catch more of their conversation. The gentlemen's voices were an intricate dance of innuendo, each phrase laced with a caution that suggested deeper truths lingered just beneath the surface.

"Lady Juliana." A voice, smooth and unyielding, cut through the lively air. Juliana turned, meeting Worthington's piercing gaze. His expression remained deceptively courteous, a mask of congeniality, yet something in the depths of his eyes sent a ripple of unease through her.

"Mr. Worthington," she greeted, her voice steady despite the tremor within. "How delightful to see you again amidst such grandeur."

"Indeed," he replied, his lips curling into a practiced smile. "I trust you are enjoying the evening? It is a splendid gathering."

"Quite so," she responded, her mind racing. "But tell me, have you perhaps encountered any rumors swirling about? They seem to cling to you like an unwelcome shadow."

His brows arched slightly, amusement mingling with calculation. "Rumors, my dear lady, are the currency of society. One must learn to navigate them or risk being swept away."

"Navigating currents is an art, wouldn't you agree?" Juliana countered, allowing her own humor to color her words. "Some currents, however, carry treacherous undertows. I find myself ever vigilant."

"Ah, vigilance is commendable," he replied smoothly, his eyes narrowing just a fraction. "Yet, it can lead to unnecessary worries."

"Or revelations," she shot back, her heart racing at the boldness of her retort. She held his gaze, challenging him without overtly revealing her intent.

As the conversation wound its way through pleasantries, Juliana's mind sought out potential allies. She spied Lady Hawthorne across the room, her shrewd nature well-known among the elite. If anyone possessed knowledge of Worthington's dubious dealings, it would be her.

"Forgive me, Mr. Worthington," she said, cutting off his next syllable with a gracious smile, "but there is a matter of urgency I must attend to. Perhaps we shall continue our discussion later?"

"Of course, Lady Juliana," he replied, though his smile did not quite reach his eyes.

With a nod, she threaded her way through the sea of elegantly dressed bodies, her resolve crystallizing with each determined step. As she approached Lady Hawthorne, she prepared herself to weave the intricate tapestry of dialogue that could potentially ensnare the truth.

"Lady Hawthorne," she began, lowering her voice to a conspiratorial whisper. "May we converse privately? There are matters regarding Mr. Worthington that weigh heavily upon my mind."

"Of course, my dear," Lady Hawthorne replied, her interest piqued. "Let us retreat to the balcony; the night air may provide clarity for troubled thoughts."

Together, they slipped away from the ballroom's clamor—two women cloaked in shadows, poised to unveil the secrets hidden behind the masks of high society.

AS THE MOON cast a silvery glow over the balcony, Lady Juliana leaned against the balustrade, her heart racing with both exhilaration and trepidation. The air was thick with the scent of blooming jasmine, mingling with the distant strains of music wafting from the ballroom. She had only just begun her inquiries into Mr. Worthington's true intentions, yet the shadows lurking around her were already beginning to take shape.

"Lady Juliana," came a smooth voice, slicing through the night like a dagger. It was Lord Ashcombe—a man whose loyalty to Worthington was well-known in their circles. His piercing blue eyes held a glint of amusement as if he found her clandestine meeting with Lady Hawthorne rather entertaining. "What secrets are you whispering about in the dark? Surely they cannot be of any consequence when one has the opportunity to dance beneath such splendid chandeliers."

"Lord Ashcombe," she replied, forcing a smile that felt more like a mask than an expression of warmth. "I assure you, it is merely a discussion of the evening's affairs. You know how we ladies delight in gossip."

"Ah, but you and I both know your interest runs deeper than idle chatter." He stepped closer, his posture exuding confidence. "Might it involve our dear Mr. Worthington? I hear rumors swirling—"

"Rumors can be dangerous," Juliana interjected, her tone cool. "It would serve one well to tread lightly, lest one finds oneself caught in a web of deceit."

"Quite poetic, my lady," he said, his voice dripping with sarcasm. "But do be careful; there are those who wouldn't hesitate to twist your words for their own gain."

She met his gaze unwaveringly, though her pulse quickened. There was a thinly veiled threat woven into his jest, and she could sense his intention was to intimidate. Yet, she refused to yield.

"Indeed," she replied, her voice steady despite the shudder running through her. "Perhaps you might share what you know of Mr. Worthington instead. After all, his motives remain an enigma to many."

Ashcombe's laughter rang out, echoing against the marble façade, but it was devoid of genuine mirth. "You would do well to remember, Lady Juliana, that curiosity can lead one down perilous paths." With that, he turned sharply on his heel, leaving her alone with the weight of his warning.

Determined not to let fear take root, Juliana returned to Lady Hawthorne, who awaited her with raised brows.

"Is everything well?" the older woman inquired, concern threading through her voice.

"Merely a reminder of the dangers lurking within our society," Juliana replied, masking her unease. "Now, tell me, have you ever heard whispers regarding Mr. Worthington's past dealings?"

"Whispers, indeed," Lady Hawthorne said, her eyes narrowing. "There are tales of his interactions with young women, those rather impressionable and vulnerable. Many believe he has a penchant for exploiting their affections for his own advantage."

"Exploiting?" Juliana repeated, her mind racing. "How so?"

"Consider the case of Miss Beatrice Langley," Lady Hawthorne continued, her tone low. "Her family faced ruin due to an unfortunate investment that Worthington orchestrated. Some say he charmed her into trusting him, only to abandon her when the tide turned."

Juliana's breath caught in her throat as the pieces began to fit together. If Worthington had indeed manipulated Miss Langley, then there might be a pattern of exploitation hidden beneath his polished exterior.

"Has there been proof?" she pressed, her resolve hardening. "Any correspondence or witness accounts?"

"None that can be publicly disclosed," Lady Hawthorne admitted. "But I suspect old letters may still exist, tucked away in the Langley estate. They might unveil more than mere whispers."

"Then we must uncover them," Juliana declared, determination surging through her veins. "If Mr. Worthington seeks to harm Reggie's family, then I shall expose him for the villain he truly is."

"Be cautious, my dear," Lady Hawthorne warned gently. "The path ahead is fraught with peril, and there are many who would protect him."

"Let them come," Juliana replied, her spirit ignited by a fierce loyalty. "I will not rest until the truth is revealed."

As they stepped back into the thrumming heart of the ball, Juliana felt invigorated. The obstacles she faced would only forge her resolve, and the looming threat of Worthington's machinations would be dismantled piece by piece.

The ballroom sparkled like a sea of stars, chandeliers casting their luminous glow upon the elegantly attired guests swirling in a calculated dance of propriety. Juliana stood at the edge of the gathering, her heart racing beneath her serene exterior.

She spied Mr. Percival Worthington across the room, his tall frame commanding attention as he engaged in conversation with a group of gentlemen, each laughter and compliment cloaking his true intentions.

Drawing in a steadying breath, she wove through the throng, her auburn hair shimmering under the lights, the soft waves brushing against her shoulders. She approached him with measured steps, her blue eyes sharp and inquisitive.

"Mr. Worthington," she greeted, her voice carrying a melodic lilt that masked her underlying urgency. "What a splendid evening we have. I trust you are enjoying your company?"

"Ah, Lady Juliana," he replied smoothly, his piercing gaze settling on her with an unsettling intensity. "Your presence makes it all the more delightful. I was just imparting some thrilling news regarding my latest investment ventures. The market is ripe for opportunity, wouldn't you agree?"

"Investment ventures?" she echoed, feigning interest while subtly probing. "I've heard whispers about your dealings with the Langley estate. I must confess, I find myself intrigued by your connections within such a venerable family."

"Connections can be quite enlightening, indeed." His smile remained polished, yet something flickered in his eyes—perhaps a glimmer of apprehension? "You know how the winds of fortune shift amongst the nobility."

"Fortune favors the bold, they say," Juliana replied, tilting her head slightly, allowing her curiosity to appear innocent. "Yet one must tread carefully. After all, vulnerable individuals often find themselves swept away in the tides of ambition."

"Quite so, but I assure you, my interests are purely benevolent." He chuckled lightly, dismissing her insinuation with a wave of his hand, though she detected a slight tightening of his jaw. "Lady Meredith St. Clair, for instance, has been a most delightful acquaintance. One might say we share a mutual admiration for culture and the arts."

"Indeed," Juliana said, her pulse quickening as she seized upon the mention of Lady Meredith. "It appears you have captivated her quite thoroughly. A woman of such refinement ought to be cherished, lest she fall prey to those with less noble intentions."

"One must always remain vigilant, my dear lady," he countered sharply, his eyes narrowing just enough to suggest irritation. "But I assure you, Lady Meredith is well aware of her own worth."

"Is she?" Juliana pressed, her resolve fortified by the weight of her suspicions. "Or has she merely become another pawn in a game played by one who knows how to manipulate the board?"

"How daring of you to suggest such things!" Worthington's laughter rang out, though it lacked warmth. "I find it rather amusing that you would presume to understand my intentions. Surely, we both know that society thrives on rumors and misunderstandings."

"Rumors often hold kernels of truth," she replied, her tone unwavering. "And I do believe the truth can be quite illuminating, especially when it concerns a lady's future."

"Ah, the future," he mused, a glint of challenge in his gaze. "A fickle thing, isn't it? Perhaps it is best left to fate?"

"Or perhaps it should be shaped by those with the courage to act," Juliana retorted, feeling the electric tension between them crackle. She had to tread carefully; this man was dangerous, adept at deflecting scrutiny.

"Touché, Lady Juliana." He bowed slightly, masking his annoyance with charm. "We shall see which of us is proven right in due course."

As the conversation waned, Juliana's mind raced. Could Lady Meredith be ensnared in Worthington's web of deceit? She resolved to investigate further, to uncover any correspondence or meetings that could reveal the truth behind their connection.

"Enjoy the rest of your evening, Mr. Worthington," she said, stepping back just enough to create distance while locking her gaze onto his, as if to pierce through his carefully constructed facade.

"Always a pleasure," he replied, his voice smooth yet tinged with a hint of menace as he watched her retreat.

Juliana turned away, her heart pounding with determination. She would not allow Worthington to manipulate those she cared for, least of all Lady Meredith. The evening was far from over; she would gather evidence, unravel the threads of his schemes, and protect those who were vulnerable to his charm. As she navigated the crowded ballroom, her mind was already formulating a plan to shine a light into the shadows of Worthington's intentions.

***

LADY JULIANA LANGDON stepped into the dimly lit drawing room of Lady Pembrum's estate, her heart racing as she scanned the gathering. The music from the ballroom wafted through the open doors, a distant echo of laughter and flirtation. Yet, in this secluded corner, shadows loomed larger than life.

"Ah, Lady Juliana," came a smooth voice, slicing through the air like a dagger. It was Miss Clara Ashworth, a socialite whose loyalty to Mr. Worthington was as notorious as her penchant for gossip. Juliana felt the weight of Clara's gaze, sharp and scrutinizing, and she clenched her hands at her sides to mask her unease.

"Miss Ashworth," Juliana replied with a practiced smile, "what a delightful evening it is." She could not afford to betray any hint of her true intentions.

"Indeed, but I fear our dear Mr. Worthington has been subject to undue scrutiny of late." Clara leaned in, her tone conspiratorial as she flicked a glance toward the ballroom. "It would be wise for you to tread carefully."

Juliana's pulse quickened, alarm bells ringing in her mind. Had Clara discovered her investigation? "I assure you, my interest lies solely in the well-being of our friends," she said, maintaining her poise, though every word felt like a delicate dance on the edge of a precipice.

"Of course," Clara replied, her lips curling into a knowing smirk. "But you must remember, some things are best left undisturbed. Curiosity can lead one down treacherous paths."

"Is that so?" Juliana feigned nonchalance, unwilling to show the turmoil brewing within her. "Perhaps it is the pursuit of truth that holds greater merit."

"Truth is often subjective, my dear." Clara's eyes glinted with a mixture of amusement and warning, and Juliana realized she was perilously close to revealing too much.

"Then I shall remain subjective in my inquiries." She turned away, forcing herself to glide past Clara, who lingered behind like a spider in a web, waiting for the unwary.

As Juliana reached the entrance to the ballroom, her breath caught in her throat. The atmosphere inside was alive, filled with swirling skirts and bright laughter. She needed information—quickly. Perhaps she would find an ally among the crowd who shared her suspicions about Worthington.

But just as she steeled herself to approach a group of acquaintances, the crackling tension in the air shifted. A footman appeared at her side, his expression grave. "My lady, a letter for you," he murmured, extending a folded note with trembling fingers.

"Who sent it?" she asked, her heart pounding as she accepted the message, the words scrawled hastily in ink.

"An anonymous source, my lady. I was instructed to deliver it directly into your hands." The footman stepped back, leaving her alone with the ominous parchment.

With trembling fingers, Juliana unfolded the letter, her eyes devouring the words:

> *Beware, Lady Juliana. Shadows gather around those who seek the light. Your inquiries have not gone unnoticed. Take heed, for danger lurks closer than you think.*

A chill raced down her spine. The stakes had risen dramatically; she was no longer merely investigating—a real threat loomed. She glanced around the ballroom, searching for familiar faces, but all she saw were masks of gaiety concealing intentions unknown.

"Very well," she whispered to herself, resolve hardening within her. With this warning etched in her mind, she would forge ahead, determined to unearth Worthington's machinations before the darkness could swallow those she cared for. She would navigate the treacherous waters of high society, ever vigilant against the lurking dangers, until the truth shone brightly enough to illuminate even the darkest corners of deceit.

THE BALLROOM THROBBED with laughter and lively conversation as Juliana maneuvered through the throng of elegantly dressed guests. Her heart raced, not from the heady atmosphere but from the urgent need to uncover the truth hidden beneath layers of deception.

"Ah, Lady Juliana! A moment of your time, if you please!" The smooth voice of Mr. Worthington pierced through the din, his presence like a shadow encroaching on her resolve. She offered a polite smile, every instinct clamoring for her to retreat, yet she stood firm, searching the room for allies.

"Mr. Worthington, how delightful to see you," she replied, her tone laced with practiced civility. "Have you seen Lord Reggie this evening? I believe he was looking for you."

"Is that so?" His eyes sparkled with cunning amusement, but Juliana sensed a deeper intent simmering beneath. "He is ever the social butterfly, flitting about while we discuss matters of great import." He leaned closer, a conspiratorial whisper escaping his lips. "I daresay, I have some intriguing news regarding the Haine family."

A flicker of alarm coursed through her. Had he already begun to weave his web of manipulation around Reggie's kin? Steeling herself, she feigned indifference, her mind racing to connect the threads of information. "Do share, Mr. Worthington. I am always eager to hear such riveting tales."

"Ah, but my dear lady," he replied, his smile sharp, "it is best discussed in more private quarters."

She stifled a shiver, a wave of trepidation crashing over her. She needed to break free from his grasp before he ensnared her further. "Perhaps another time," she said, stepping back. "I have business with Lady Ellingham. A matter of utmost importance."

"Business, indeed," he murmured, tilting his head slightly, an inscrutable glint in his eye. She turned away, navigating the crowd until she found refuge by the grand staircase. Leaning against the polished wood, she took a steadying breath, her thoughts whirling.

Through careful observation, she had pieced together fragments of conversations and whispered rumors. It was then, amidst the noise, that she spotted a familiar figure—Miss Ashworth—engaged in hushed discourse with a gentleman clad in somber attire. Curiosity ignited within her, propelling her forward.

As she drew closer, Juliana strained to overhear. "...the documents are secure, but it would be unwise to underestimate him," Miss Ashworth cautioned, her voice tinged with urgency. "If Worthington learns of our plans, there will be consequences."

Juliana's breath caught. The documents! They must contain damning evidence against Reggie's family. With stealth, she edged nearer, her pulse hammering in her ears.

"Rest assured, my lady, they shall remain undisclosed," the man replied. "But the whispers grow louder; we cannot afford to wait much longer."

"Indeed," Miss Ashworth said, her brow furrowing. "We must act before he can ruin us all."

In that moment, clarity struck. This was the key—the very evidence she had sought to expose Worthington's true intentions. Gathering her wits, she slipped away unnoticed, clutching the knowledge like a precious jewel.

Once safely distanced from prying eyes, Juliana pressed herself against the cool wall of a secluded corridor, her mind racing with implications. What would be the repercussions of revealing such information? The delicate balance of loyalty and duty weighed heavily upon her shoulders.

"To protect them," she whispered to herself, "I must tread carefully."

Her thoughts darted through the ramifications: exposing Worthington could bring ruin upon Reggie's family, yet allowing his schemes to unfold unchecked would spell disaster. Each option bore its own peril.

With resolute determination, she began plotting her next steps, crafting a strategy that would utilize the very evidence she had gleaned. She would need to gather allies—those who understood the stakes involved. The intricate dance of high society required subtlety, and she would navigate it with the grace expected of her station.

"Yes, I shall act," she muttered under her breath, her blue eyes shimmering with purpose. "But first, I must ensure my footing is secure." As she moved toward the ballroom once more, resolve ignited within her. Whatever storm lay ahead, she would face it head-on, armed with the truth and a heart steadfast in its mission to protect those she loved.

THE BALLROOM BUZZED with the fervent energy of London's elite, chandeliers casting a warm glow over polished floors and gilded decor. Juliana stood near the grand fireplace, her heart pounding like a wild stallion as she observed Mr. Percival Worthington, resplendent in his tailored coat, weaving through clusters of guests with practiced ease.

"Juliana," whispered Lady Beatrice, urgency lacing her voice, "are you certain about this?"

"Quite," Juliana replied, her gaze locked on Worthington. The weight of her evidence felt like a vice around her chest, but she would not falter now. She had come too far.

With a deep breath, Juliana straightened her spine and glided toward the center of the room, her presence commanding attention. Conversations dwindled, curious eyes turning towards her as she approached the man who had so deftly entwined himself within their lives.

"Mr. Worthington!" she called out, her voice ringing clear above the murmurs. The crowd parted, anticipation thickening the air.

He turned, surprise flickering across his sharp features before he masked it with a charming smile. "Lady Juliana, what a delightful surprise."

"Delightful indeed," she countered, her tone steady, though her pulse quickened. "I believe our acquaintances are owed a revelation regarding your true intentions."

"True intentions?" Worthington feigned confusion, yet his eyes narrowed slightly, calculating.

"Yes," Juliana pressed on, gathering the strength she needed. "You have woven a web of deceit that threatens the good name of the Duke of Messingham and his family." She stepped closer, the surrounding whispers intensifying. "Your manipulations have not gone unnoticed."

"How dramatic, my dear," he retorted, smooth as silk, but the tremor in his voice was unmistakable. "Surely, you must possess no evidence to substantiate such wild claims?"

"On the contrary," she said, pulling a folded letter from her glove, raising it high for all to see. "This correspondence reveals your scheme—a vile plot to undermine the Duke of Messingham and gain favor among those less scrupulous than yourself."

Gasps echoed in the hall, and Juliana felt the tide shift; curiosity morphed into outrage. She continued, each word chosen with precision, infusing them with righteous indignation. "It is no mere coincidence that your affections towards Lady Meredith coincide with your sudden interest in the Messingham estate. Do you think we will stand idly by while you exploit our society's trust?"

Worthington purred, attempting to regain control, "Your passion blinds you to reason. This is a grave accusation—one that could ruin your standing as well. In fact, I have sent a letter to the Duke with my findings as of late."

Juliana looked at him cross. "Do tell," she said, thinking he had nothing.

Worthington sneered, "That there is no such person as *'Henri de Beaumont'*."

Ten

Juliana hesitated at the threshold of the drawing room, her heart drumming furiously against her chest. The lavish decor loomed around her—golden-framed portraits glaring down from the walls, sumptuous silk drapes framing tall windows that overlooked the manicured gardens outside. Each detail of the opulence seemed to mock her turmoil. She took a tentative step forward, her hand brushing against the cool marble mantle, grounding herself momentarily before she ventured further into the gilded cage of societal expectation.

"Juliana!" The voice sliced through the air like a blade, and her breath caught in her throat. The Duke of Messingham stood near the grand fireplace, his expression a tempest of betrayal. "What is the meaning of this charade?"

She swallowed hard, the weight of his piercing green eyes pinning her in place. *How could she explain?* The very foundation of their friendship felt as though it were crumbling beneath her feet. "Reggie, I—"

"Do not dare to call me that," he interrupted, his voice taut with fury. Each word dripped with disappointment, unraveling the threadbare fabric of trust they had woven together since childhood. His posture was rigid; fists clenched at his sides, he appeared both regal and shattered—a young man grappling with the enormity of her deception.

"Why did you not confide in me?" Reggie's tone shifted, an undercurrent of vulnerability surfacing, yet it was drowned in the swell of his anger. "You have spun a web of lies, and for what? To shield me from the truth?" He stepped closer, his gaze unwavering. "Do you take me for a fool?"

"Reggie, please." The tremor in her voice betrayed her resolve. "I never meant to hurt you." Her fingers fidgeted at her side, betraying her discomfort as she sought the words to mend the rift wrought by her choices. "There are reasons, circumstances beyond my control—"

"Ah, circumstances!" he spat, cutting her off. "You speak of them as if they absolve you. Your secrecy speaks volumes, Juliana. What do you think I am? A mere pawn in your dangerous game?"

"That is not fair!" she protested, the plea emerging with a fervor that startled even her. "I acted out of necessity—not malice. You must understand—"

"Understand?" His face was taut, jaw clenched so tightly it might shatter. "You think I can simply comprehend your treachery? That the years we've spent together mean nothing to you?"

Each accusation struck her like arrows, piercing deep into the core of her being. Juliana's composure wavered as she grappled with her guilt. *How could she possibly convey the tumultuous feelings swirling within her?* The love, the fear, and the burden of duty weighed heavily upon her soul. Desperation clawed at her throat, but the gravity of the moment kept her rooted to the spot. *Would he ever forgive her?*

"Reggie," Juliana's voice faltered, a delicate whisper against the backdrop of their tense standoff. She took a tentative step forward, the plush carpet beneath her feet feeling like a treacherous sea. Her heart raced, unsteady and frantic, as she searched his emerald eyes for any semblance of understanding.

"Do not feign innocence!" he barked, fists clenched at his sides, tension coiling in his posture. The firelight flickered, casting shadows across his chiseled features—a visage torn between fury and disbelief. "You owe me the truth."

"Then let me speak." Her breath hitched, an emotion too raw to contain bubbling beneath the surface. "I love you, Reggie. I have loved you for years." The confession poured out, mingling with the air heavy with anticipation. Her gaze remained locked on his, searching for a flicker of warmth amid the storm raging within him.

"Love?" His skepticism was palpable, his brow furrowing deeper. "Is that what you call this charade? A fabricated engagement? How could you stand before me with such deceit?"

Juliana's voice trembled, each word weighed down by guilt. "Damn that Worthington—I never intended to deceive you. My family's expectations…" She hesitated, swallowing hard as the truth clawed its way to the forefront. "They were suffocating. My father insisted upon a match with Lord Pembrum—a man who does not hold my heart. I sought to escape that fate. To protect you from being entwined in my family's schemes."

"Protect me?" Reggie's tone dripped with incredulity, his fists loosening slightly but still taut with suppressed emotion. "You think I needed protection from you? From the very woman I believed I could trust above all others?"

"Trust?" Her voice cracked, pain lacing her words. "That is precisely what I shattered. But my intentions were not born from malice. I thought—"

"Thought what?" His voice lowered, simmering just beneath the surface, a tempest held at bay. "You thought I would simply accept your lies?"

"That if I shielded you from the truth, it might spare us both heartache." She stepped closer, her heart pounding in rhythm with the desperation in her chest. "I see now how foolish I was. You deserve honesty, Reggie. But I could not bear the thought of losing you to a life of duty and obligation."

For a moment, silence wrapped around them like a shroud, thick and suffocating. Reggie's expression shifted, conflict dancing in his green eyes. The anger ebbed, replaced by a vulnerability that mirrored her own. Yet the hurt lingered, etching lines of uncertainty across his brow.

"Juliana…" he began, voice strained, grappling with the whirlwind of emotions swirling within him. "How am I to reconcile this betrayal with the love I feel for you?"

"By allowing me to show you," she pleaded, her voice gaining strength as determination ignited within her. "Let me prove that my feelings are genuine. That I would choose you over any societal expectation."

But even as the words left her lips, she saw the struggle in his eyes—the fine line he walked between longing and caution. She felt the weight of their shared history pressing down, a reminder of the bond they had forged since childhood, now threatened by the rift of her misjudgment. Would he allow love to conquer the doubts burrowing deep within him?

The air in the drawing room grew thicker, a palpable tension hanging between Juliana and Reggie like a drawn bowstring. Lady Beatrice stepped forward, her presence a soothing balm amidst the rising storm. With a practiced grace, she placed herself between them, her warm brown eyes darting from one to the other.

"Reggie, Juliana," she began, her voice calm yet firm, "you must both acknowledge the weight of your words and actions." Her gaze held them captive, urging them to heed her counsel. "This moment is fraught with consequence, not only for yourselves but for those who care for you."

"Consequences?" Reggie's voice cracked, a mixture of pain and indignation swirling within it. He clenched his fists tighter, as if he could contain the turmoil inside him. "And what of my feelings, Lady Beatrice? What of trust?"

"Exactly," Juliana interjected, her heart racing as she turned toward Lady Beatrice. "I never meant for any of this to happen!"

"Enough!" Lady Beatrice raised her hand gently, her demeanor unyielding despite the emotional tempest around her. "Both of you must listen. There are obligations that extend beyond yourselves, ties that bind you to family and reputation. Think of the lives intertwined with your own."

Reggie's furrowed brow deepened, the conflict still raging in his eyes. "And what do you suggest, Lady Beatrice? That I simply forget the betrayal? That we ignore how easily trust can shatter?"

"That is not what I imply," she replied with measured clarity. "But rather that you consider the path forward together. You both deserve happiness, yet it must be tempered by understanding—"

"Understanding?" Lady Catherine's voice cut through the air like a blade, sharp and resolute. She entered the conversation with an unmistakable authority, her silver-streaked hair gleaming under the chandelier. "Let us not forget the expectations that govern our society, Beatrice." Her piercing blue eyes swept over the pair, assessing their expressions with a maternal scrutiny. "Your actions have repercussions, Juliana, not merely on your own heart but on the Haine name as well. Are you prepared to bear that burden?"

"Lady Catherine, please," Juliana implored, desperation lacing her tone. "This was all borne from a place of fear. I wanted to protect us both from a fate dictated by duty alone."

"Yet in doing so, you have placed yourself in a most precarious position," Lady Catherine stated firmly, her demeanor unyielding. "You must understand, my dear, that reputation is everything in our world. One misstep, one whisper among the ton, and the damage is irreparable."

"Then what am I to do?" Juliana's voice trembled as she searched for solace in Reggie's eyes, longing for understanding amidst the chaos. "If love is not enough to overcome these obstacles, then what hope do we truly possess?"

"Hope lies in transparency and commitment," Lady Beatrice interjected again, her tone softening. "Only from honesty can you weave a future worth aspiring to. Both of you must decide whether you are willing to brave the storm together—or allow it to tear you apart."

As silence enveloped them once more, Juliana felt the weight of their words settle heavily upon her shoulders. The stakes had never been higher, yet buried beneath the turmoil stirred a flicker of determination.

* * *

THE HEAVY SILENCE that had settled in the drawing room was pierced by the sharp click of Mr. Worthington's boots on the polished floor, his tall figure emerging from the shadows like a predator circling its prey. He wore a sardonic smile, his piercing eyes gleaming with a mixture of amusement and malice.

"Ah, Lady Juliana," he began, his voice smooth as silk yet edged with an underlying threat, "one cannot help but marvel at the tangled web you've woven. It is most intriguing, truly. But tell me, have you considered the ramifications of your little charade? The whispers, the scandal—it can all unravel rather swiftly." He leaned forward slightly, the glint of mischief dancing across his features. "Your reputation, so carefully cultivated, could crumble under the weight of such deception."

Juliana's stomach twisted at his words, but she refused to yield to the tide of anxiety threatening to drown her. Instead, she straightened her spine, drawing strength from the resolve that flickered within her. She would not allow him to manipulate her any further.

"Mr. Worthington," she replied, her voice steady despite the tumult within, "you speak of reputations as if they are but trinkets to be bartered. What you fail to recognize is that true worth lies beyond mere appearances. You thrive on chaos, don't you?" Her blue eyes narrowed defiantly, locking onto his with fierce determination. "Your intentions are clear—sow discord and watch others fall into disarray."

His expression shifted, momentarily caught off guard by her unexpected boldness, but he quickly masked it behind a veneer of charm. "Why, my dear, I simply offer a candid observation. One must tread carefully in these waters, lest one finds themselves drowned in scandal."

"Scandal?" she echoed, her voice rising, echoing through the lavish room adorned with gilded frames and velvet drapery. "You parade around as if concern for reputation drives your every word, yet your true motivation is self-interest, cloaked in false camaraderie. You relish the power of suggestion, wielding it like a dagger."

"Is that so?" he countered, feigning innocence. "And what do you propose, then? That one should simply disregard the consequences of their actions?"

"One should embrace honesty instead of deceit," she insisted, her heart racing as she pressed on. "It is far more honorable to confront the truth than to hide behind veiled threats, Mr. Worthington. Your attempts to manipulate this situation will not work on me. I see you for what you truly are—a man who revels in the suffering of others."

Gasps rippled through the room, followed by an almost tangible hush. Juliana stood firm, feeling the weight of every gaze upon her, but emboldened by the knowledge that she had spoken her truth. She would not allow Worthington's cunning to dictate her fate any longer.

"Perhaps you should consider your own position," he shot back, his voice laced with venom. "A lady who challenges societal norms may find herself quite alone when the music stops."

"Alone?" she retorted, meeting his stare unflinchingly. "I stand with my convictions, and that is a far greater comfort than your hollow alliances."

In that moment, amidst the ornate splendor of the drawing room, a palpable shift occurred. The tension crackled in the air, leaving no doubt that the balance of power had shifted. Juliana felt the stirrings of hope ignite within her chest;

perhaps, just perhaps, she could carve out her own destiny amidst the ruins of treachery.

The room hung in a breathless silence, the flickering candlelight casting shadows on the opulent wallpaper as Juliana stood her ground against Mr. Worthington. Her heart raced, yet within that storm of emotion, she felt a clarity she had never known before. The weight of his threats loomed heavy, but she bore it bravely, her chin raised defiantly.

Reggie leaned against the doorframe, his earlier fury now eclipsed by an unexpected admiration. He watched as Juliana's blue eyes blazed with a fierce determination, their depths reflecting not only courage but the vulnerability she so often concealed. The tension in the air was palpable; he could almost feel the energy shift, swirling around her like an invisible cloak of strength.

"Do you truly believe you can manipulate me?" she challenged, her voice unwavering. "I see through your charade, Mr. Worthington, and I will not allow you to dictate my fate."

Each word struck Reggie with equal force, igniting a fire in his chest. He had witnessed many a lady wilt under pressure, yet here stood Juliana—unyielding, fierce. The contrast between her delicate frame and the strength of her resolve captivated him, pulling him closer even as his mind wrestled with the implications of her defiance.

"Your bravery is commendable," he murmured under his breath, though whether it was meant for himself or her, he could not say.

"Perhaps you should reflect on your own position, Lady Juliana," Worthington sneered, his voice slick with condescension. The corners of his mouth turned up mockingly, but he faltered when faced with the unwavering intensity of Juliana's gaze.

"Enough!" Reggie finally interjected, stepping forward, his voice firm and commanding. The room seemed to exhale as all eyes turned toward him, the atmosphere charged with unspoken tension. Yet, it was not just anger he felt; it was a burgeoning respect for Juliana that compelled him.

"Lady Beatrice," he called, seeking the steady presence of Juliana's sister, who stood nearby, her fingers clasped together in quiet concern. "What counsel can you provide? This situation demands clarity."

Lady Beatrice moved forward, her warm brown eyes assessing the charged faces around her. She exuded calmness, a beacon of wisdom amidst the tumult. "Juliana, Reggie," she began, her voice rich and soothing, "this matter is fraught with complications, yet it also presents an opportunity—a chance to unveil your true desires."

"Desires?" Worthington scoffed, but Lady Beatrice silenced him with a look, her authority leaving no room for dissent.

"Consider what stands before you," she continued, her gaze shifting between them. "You both possess the power to shape your own futures. But first, you must understand what you truly want, away from the expectations of society and the malicious intent of others."

Reggie felt the weight of her words settle over him like a shroud. His thoughts flashed to the moments he had shared with Juliana—the laughter, the stolen glances, the connection that seemed to pulse between them like a living thing. Did he dare to hope for something more?

"Juliana," he said, his voice softer now, "what do you seek amidst this turmoil?"

Juliana hesitated, the vulnerability of the moment wrapping around her like a fragile veil. The space between them thrummed with unvoiced possibilities. Though the world outside might conspire against them, within this drawing room, perhaps they could find freedom in their own truth.

* * *

LADY JULIANA LANGDON stood at the center of the opulent drawing room, her heart racing in response to the tumultuous emotions swirling within her. The heavy drapes framed the windows, filtering the late afternoon light into a soft golden hue, and yet it felt as though a storm brewed inside her, threatening to break free. She straightened her spine, willing herself to meet Reggie's piercing green gaze.

"Reggie," she began, her voice trembling but resolute, "I cannot allow the weight of deception to govern my heart any longer." Each word was laden with the gravity of her confession, echoing like a bell tolling through the stillness of the room.

His brow furrowed, the remnants of anger flickering across his features, but beneath it lay something softer—a glimmer of hope, perhaps? Juliana pressed onward, emboldened by the vulnerability that had been forged in the crucible of confrontation. "I love you, Reggie. I have loved you for as long as I can remember. My actions stemmed from fear—fear of losing you and fear of societal expectation."

The silence that followed was palpable, stretching out like a taut string ready to snap. Reggie's expression shifted; the tightness around his mouth softened, revealing uncertainty masked by pride. Juliana's heart pounded as she observed the battle waging behind his eyes, the clash of longing and hesitation reflected in their depths.

"Juliana..." His voice was low, almost a whisper, laden with the weight of unspoken truths. He stepped closer, the air between them charged with an electric tension, and she could feel her breath hitch in her throat.

"Do you not see?" she implored, desperation creeping into her tone. "What I did was foolish, yes, but only because I feared being without you. I sought to protect our bond, even if it meant shrouding it in lies." Her words flowed forth, earnest and raw, as if peeling back the layers of her guarded heart.

Reggie remained silent for a moment, the turmoil within him evident in the way his fists clenched and unclenched at his sides. And then, as if the storm had subsided, he exhaled slowly, his gaze unwavering. "You must know," he said, his voice steadying, "that you are the very essence of my dreams, and it pains me to think you felt compelled to fabricate such a pretense."

"Then we are united in our desire," she breathed, her pulse quickening as she sensed the shift in him. "We need not bow to the whims of others. Together, we can forge our own path."

Reggie's eyes deepened, shimmering with emotion. "I have long deflected my true feelings, fearing they would burden you. But now, I can no longer deny it." He took another step closer, closing the distance between them. "I love you, Juliana. Through all the chaos, you remain my greatest joy."

The sincerity of his admission washed over her, soothing the jagged edges of her guilt. Juliana felt a rush of warmth bloom in her chest, the tender balm of his words wrapping around her heart like a protective embrace. She dared to hope—for herself, for them—amidst the turbulence of societal expectations and familial duties.

"Then let us speak of our future, unencumbered by shame or deceit," she murmured, her voice imbued with newfound conviction. In that moment, the world beyond the drawing room faded into insignificance, leaving only the two of them standing at the precipice of possibility, their hearts laid bare before one another.

Juliana felt the world around her dissolve as Reggie stepped forward, his imposing presence drawing her in. She trembled slightly, not from fear but from an electrifying anticipation that coursed through her veins. The air thickened with unspoken words and desires, and without a moment's hesitation, she closed the distance between them.

Their bodies collided, an urgent embrace that spoke of longing and desperation. Juliana nestled against him, feeling the warmth of his frame envelop her like a shield against the chaos outside their cocoon. His arms encircled her waist, firm yet tender, grounding her in an instant of truth. She inhaled the familiar scent of him—woodsmoke mingling with the crispness of linen—and it ignited something deep within her.

"Reggie," she breathed, lost in the depths of his piercing green eyes that now shimmered with vulnerability. Every worry, every doubt about their future faded as their hearts beat in synchrony, a wild rhythm echoing the fervor of their emotions. They were no longer just Lady Juliana Langdon and the Duke of Messingham; they were two souls intertwined, yearning for one another amidst societal expectations that threatened to tear them apart.

"God, Juliana," he murmured, his voice thick with longing as he pressed his forehead against hers. "We have fought this for too long."

"Then let us stop fighting," she replied, a fierce determination rising within her. She tilted her chin up, searching his face, desperate for affirmation. "Let us embrace what we feel."

As if compelled by some unseen force, Reggie leaned in, capturing her lips with his own. The kiss was fervent, raw—a release of all the restraint they had forced upon themselves. Time blurred, and the grand drawing room faded into oblivion. In that moment, there was nothing but the taste of each other and a promise of love that had endured despite the trials they faced.

The passionate embrace consumed them, leaving no space for doubt. Yet, as they pulled away reluctantly, breathless and wide-eyed, the reality of their situation crept back in, heavy and undeniable. The opulent surroundings felt stifling, their gilded frames and silken drapery bearing witness to their scandalous union.

"Lady Catherine," Juliana whispered, a flicker of anxiety threading through her heart as she turned her gaze toward the formidable figure standing at the edge of the room. The matriarch's sharp blue eyes regarded them with a mixture of concern and resignation, as if she had witnessed the very fabric of her family's future unraveling before her.

"Juliana, Reggie," Lady Catherine began, her voice steady yet laced with a weight of authority. "I cannot pretend to be blind to the depth of your feelings." Her regal posture remained unwavering, though her expression softened just enough to reveal the turmoil beneath. "Yet, you must understand the implications of such a union. Society will not forgive easily."

"Mother," Reggie interjected, his brow furrowing in frustration. "We care not for society's judgment. Our love is true."

"True, yes," Lady Catherine acknowledged, her tone reflective. "But our reputation, my dear son, is precariously built upon the perceptions of those around us. In the eyes of others, you have been engaged to Lady St. Clair. You both stand at a precipice, and I... I can only hope to safeguard you from the inevitable fallout."

Juliana's heart raced, uncertainty flooding her veins. *Would their newfound love withstand the scrutiny of the ton?* Yet, as she met Reggie's gaze, she found strength in the unwavering resolve reflected there.

"Then let us navigate it together," Juliana declared, her voice resolute. "With your guidance, Lady Catherine, we shall prove that love can triumph over the shackles of expectation."

"Very well," Lady Catherine said, a reluctant acceptance settling in her features. "If your hearts are set upon this course, I vow to protect your reputation. Reggie, my dear son, you must see Lady St. Clair immediately."

Eleven

THE NEXT MORNING

Juliana stood near the grand window of the Langdon estate, her fingers tracing the delicate lace of her sleeve as she stared out at the meticulously manicured gardens beyond. The sun dipped low, casting an amber glow that illuminated the petals of blooming roses, yet she felt no warmth from it. The vibrant colors mocked the dull ache within her heart.

"Juliana?" Beatrice's voice broke through the silence, soft yet aware, as she entered the room. She approached with measured steps, concern etched upon her features. "You are here alone. Why not join me in the parlor? I have prepared tea."

"I fear I might shatter like glass if I attempt to engage," Juliana replied, her tone barely above a whisper. The prospect of forced gaiety felt insurmountable, each word a reminder of what she had lost.

Beatrice placed a gentle hand on her shoulder, a grounding presence amidst the storm of emotions swirling inside Juliana. "It is understandable to wish for solitude, but sometimes, sharing burdens can lighten their weight."

"Perhaps," she conceded, her voice trembling. "But how does one share such pain without appearing foolish?"

"By being honest." Beatrice's gaze was unwavering, her brown eyes filled with empathy. "What weighs most heavily upon your heart, dear sister?"

The question lingered, drawing forth a torrent of thoughts that threatened to overwhelm her. "I loved him, Beatrice. Truly, deeply." The confession hung between them, heavy and palpable. "Yet he will choose duty over love, and I... I cannot comprehend how one moves forward after such a betrayal."

"We know not yet of his choice, dear. And besides, his choice does not reflect your worth," Beatrice interjected gently. "Reggie carries the weight of expectations that bind him. It is a burden you cannot bear for him."

"Does that make it any easier to endure?" Juliana's voice cracked, frustration mingling with sorrow. "I wanted our future—our children, our laughter echoing through halls like these. Now, it feels like a cruel jest, a mirage that has vanished before my very eyes."

"Life often presents us with paths we do not choose," Beatrice replied, her tone steady and soothing. "But you must remember, even in loss, there lies the seed of something new. What if this heartbreak leads you to discover parts of yourself previously hidden?"

"Discover what?" Juliana scoffed bitterly, the sound hollow in her throat. "A life devoid of love?"

"Not devoid of love," Beatrice corrected softly, leaning closer, her warmth inviting. "Just different. You are strong, Juliana. Stronger than you give yourself credit for. This moment will not define you; it's merely a chapter in your story."

"How can I be brave when all I feel is despair?" Juliana's vulnerability laid bare, her eyes glistening with unshed tears. "There was a future painted in hues of joy, and now it is all shades of gray."

"Then let me help you paint anew," Beatrice urged, her grip tightening reassuringly. "You are not alone in this; I shall stand by your side. Together, we will find the vibrancy again, even if it takes time."

"Time," Juliana echoed, the word heavy on her tongue. "Will time ever heal this wound? In order to be by side, he must break an engagement."

"Yes," Beatrice affirmed, her voice imbued with hope. "But know that you are deserving of happiness, even if it feels elusive at present."

"Your words grant me solace," Juliana admitted, her heart swelling with gratitude despite the bleakness. A flicker of resolve ignited within her. "I shall strive to honor my feelings but also seek the strength to rise."

Juliana turned away from the comforting embrace of her sister, her heart still heavy with the weight of Reggie's potential decision. The walls of the Langdon estate loomed around her, familiar yet suffocating in their grandeur. Each step she took down the polished corridor felt as if it echoed her despair—an endless refrain of loss reverberating against the marble floors.

"Juliana...," Beatrice called softly, but the gentle sound faded behind her as Juliana pressed on. She needed solace, a sanctuary where the turmoil within could be contained, if only for a moment. Her fingers brushed against the cool, ornate banister as she ascended the staircase, seeking refuge in her room, the one place where the world outside could not intrude upon her thoughts.

Upon entering her chamber, Juliana closed the door with a sigh that seemed to catch in her throat. The familiar scent of lavender lingered in the air, mingling with the faint aroma of dust and aged wood. It was a quiet haven, adorned with delicate lace curtains and a plush chaise lounge draped with her favorite shawl. Yet, even this sanctuary felt marred by the remnants of her shattered dreams.

She crossed the room, each footfall deliberate, as if she were afraid of disturbing the fragile peace that surrounded her. The sunlight filtered through the gauzy fabric, casting dappled patterns upon the floor—a stark contrast to the storm brewing within her heart. With a trembling hand, she reached for the chair beside her writing desk, settling into its embrace as though it might hold her together.

How can I move forward when my heart remains tethered to him? she thought, the question echoing against the stillness. In her mind, Reggie's piercing green eyes flashed before her, full of unspoken words and promises now lost to the winds of duty.

She fought against the swell of emotion, inhaling deeply as if to quell the rising tide of grief.

But the truth clawed at her insides. His choice had been made, borne from a sense of obligation she could not fault him for, yet it left her feeling adrift as if cast upon an unforgiving ocean. *To respect his decision,* she thought again. *What does that mean for me? To bury my feelings beneath the weight of his family's expectations?*

The thought gnawed at her like a persistent ache. Could she truly find happiness without him, or would her heart remain forever bound to the specter of what might have been? She ran her fingers through her auburn hair, pulling it back as if that simple act could untangle the mess of emotions swirling within.

"Am I to become merely a shadow of my former self?" she questioned aloud, staring into the mirror that reflected her weary countenance. The vibrant blue of her eyes seemed dulled, shrouded in a haze of sorrow. The reflection gazed back with uncertainty, mirroring the internal conflict that raged beneath her composed exterior.

"Perhaps time will grant me clarity," she said, her voice faltering. "Or perhaps it will only deepen the wounds." Heat pricked at the corners of her eyes, but she blinked fiercely, refusing to surrender to tears once more.

With a determined breath, Juliana rose from her seat, pacing the confines of her room, her movements swift and restless. The very air felt thick with the weight of her heartache, yet within that turmoil, a flicker of resolve began to emerge. She would honor her love for Reggie, but she could not allow it to consume her entirely.

"To live is to choose, and I must choose myself," she declared quietly, the conviction growing stronger with every beat of her heart. Yet, as the shadows lengthened across the walls, she wrestled with the haunting question: could she truly forge a new path while the echoes of her love for him lingered like ghostly whispers in the corners of her mind?

JULIANA STEPPED into the grand foyer of the Langdon estate, her heart heavy as the weight of her potential loss settled upon her like a shroud. The marble floors gleamed under the soft glow of crystal chandeliers, their light refracted in a dazzling display across the polished surfaces. Ornate tapestries hung on the walls, each thread woven with tales of glory and triumph, yet now felt mocking against the tumult within her spirit.

Her fingers brushed against the cool banister as she ascended the sweeping staircase, each step resonating with a hollow echo. The walls loomed tall and regal, adorned with portraits of ancestors who seemed to gaze down with disapproving eyes, as if judging her for the turmoil that threatened to unravel her carefully maintained composure. In the sanctuary of her room, she longed for solace but found only a reminder of the dreams that now lay shattered.

As she entered her chamber, the opulence enveloped her—the delicate lace curtains framing the window fluttered gently in the breeze, and the silken upholstery of her chaise lounge beckoned for rest. Yet, the beauty of her surroundings felt surreal, a gilded cage that trapped her aching heart. She sank onto the edge of the bed, her hands knotting in her lap as she fought against the tide of emotions threatening to drown her.

"How can I let go?" she whispered to the air, her voice barely rising above the whisper of the wind outside. "How can I move forward when my heart remains tethered to him?"

The memories of Reggie flooded her mind—his laughter that danced in the air like music, the way his piercing green eyes had held her gaze, promising a future that now crumbled beneath her feet. A sharp pang gripped her chest, and she pressed her palm against it, willing the pain to subside.

"To honor his choice is to betray my own heart," she pondered aloud, her forehead resting against the cool glass of the windowpane. Outside, the gardens sprawled in vibrant hues, a riot of color that contrasted sharply with the grayness that clouded her thoughts. The rosebushes swayed gently, their blossoms unfurling with abandon, while she felt herself wilting, stifled by her heartache.

"Perhaps I must accept this burden," she murmured, drawing strength from the very air that filled the room. Her resolve began to solidify like iron forged in fire. Reggie's decision, painful though it was, did not erase the love she bore for him; rather, it demanded that she find a new path, one paved with resilience.

"To live is to endure," Juliana whispered, straightening her spine as she turned from the window, her gaze settling on her reflection in the ornate mirror. The auburn waves of her hair framed her face, and for the first time that day, she allowed herself a flicker of determination. Though her heart may ache, she would not be defined by her sorrow.

"Let them see me whole," she resolved, a sense of purpose igniting within her. She would forge ahead, even if the journey was steeped in shadows. With a deep breath, she smoothed her skirts and stepped back into the world beyond her door, ready to face whatever awaited her.

Twelve

A FEW DAYS LATER

The door to Lady Juliana's chamber creaked softly as she sank into the solitary embrace of her chair, a heavy silence settling around her like a shroud. With trembling hands, she pressed her face into her palms, the weight of despair pressing down harder than the finest silk gowns draped upon her slender form. The moonlight filtered through the filmy curtains, casting ghostly shadows that danced across the ornate wallpaper, yet all beauty faded into a distant memory as her heartache consumed her.

There were no letters, no whispers ... she hadn't heard from Reggie in a few days.

A muffled sob escaped her lips, swallowed by the delicate handkerchief clasped in her grasp. The fabric felt damp and unforgiving against her skin, absorbing every tear that dared to escape. She clutched it tighter, her knuckles turning white as though she might strangle the very emotions that threatened to drown her. Each breath came shallow, hitching in her throat, as if the air itself conspired to suffocate her sorrow.

"Why must it be this way?" she murmured, though the question hung unanswered in the stillness of the room. She felt the cold touch of loneliness wrap around her, an uninvited companion that whispered of hopelessness. The world outside continued its relentless march, but within these four walls, time stood still, leaving her stranded in a moment of unrelenting grief.

Her thoughts flitted like moths to a flame, darting from one painful memory to another—each one a reminder of the love she feared she would never claim. The echoes of laughter from the ballroom seemed to mock her isolation, a cruel jest by fate herself. And yet, with each heartbeat, she longed for something—someone—to pull her from this abyss.

Juliana drew the handkerchief closer, pressing it against her eyes as the fresh wave of tears broke free. She felt utterly alone, a fragile flower wilting in a garden bereft of sunlight. But within the cocoon of her anguish, a flicker of resilience sparked deep inside her; a yearning to break through the pain and reach for a different tomorrow.

"Reggie," she breathed, the name a bittersweet balm and poison alike. If only he were here, she thought, if only he could see the tempest raging within her chest. Perhaps then, the distance between them would dissolve, and she would no longer need to mourn what might have been.

Yet, for now, all she had was the empty room and the handkerchief stained with her silent lament.

With a sudden resolve, Juliana thrust the handkerchief from her face and sprang to her feet. The wooden floorboards creaked beneath her as she paced, each step echoing the turmoil that churned within her heart. The air was thick with the weight of her despair, heavy like the satin draperies framing her window—a constant reminder of the life outside that seemed to mock her sorrow.

"Will he? Has he?" she murmured, her voice barely above a whisper. The question lingered in the air, taunting her. Reggie, with his easy laughter and dazzling smile, had captivated the hearts of many, yet here she stood, shackled by insecurities that clawed at her mind. She paused mid-stride, a hand pressed to her chest as if to still the frantic beating within. Thoughts of his impending marriage to Lady St. Clair gnawed at her. *How could she compete with the likes of someone so perfectly polished, so effortlessly charming?*

"Am I doomed to watch from the sidelines?" The words escaped her lips like a lament, filled with bitterness and longing. She resumed her restless pacing, her breaths coming in short gasps as visions of their shared moments flickered before her eyes—dancing beneath the twinkling chandeliers, stolen glances across crowded ballrooms, whispers of sweet promises exchanged under the boughs of the ancient oak in the garden.

"Will he even remember those moments when he is wed?" she questioned, the idea striking deeper than any blade. With each turn, her anguish mounted, swirling around her like a tempest. She longed to grasp the love they once shared, but the thought of losing him forever paralyzed her.

"Why must duty dictate the course of my heart?" Her voice rose, trembling with frustration. She halted at her vanity, staring at the reflection of a woman who looked poised yet felt utterly defeated. The delicate lace of her gown seemed a mockery in this moment of vulnerability.

"Juliana," she chastised herself, "you are no stranger to hardship. Do not yield to despair." Yet, the strength of her own words faltered against the tides of uncertainty crashing over her. She pressed her palms against the cool surface of the mahogany desk, seeking stability in its steadfastness as her thoughts spiraled further into turmoil.

"Perhaps I am destined to remain an afterthought in his life," she concluded, her heart sinking. Desperation clawed at her throat, tightening until she could scarcely breathe. The elegant room, adorned with fine art and treasures, felt more like a gilded cage than a haven.

"Enough!" she cried out, startling herself. The echo of her voice filled the silence, and she realized then that she could no longer bear the burden of inaction. If love were to triumph, it required courage—an audacity she must summon within herself. She took a deep breath, steeling her resolve, and continued her restless march, determined to confront the truth of her feelings, come what may.

With a sudden swell of emotion, Juliana halted her restless pacing and turned toward the window, the pale moon casting its silvery glow across her chamber. The glass pane felt cool against her fingertips as she leaned closer, peering out into the night. The garden beyond lay shrouded in shadows, the once vibrant blooms now mere silhouettes under the celestial light.

A soft breeze stirred the leaves, whispering secrets of the world outside—a world that seemed to pulse with life, yet felt achingly distant.

"Reggie," she breathed, her voice barely more than a sigh. The very name held a warmth that contrasted sharply with the chill in her heart. How she longed for his presence, for the laughter they shared, for the moments when the weight of societal expectations faded into nothingness. Without him, solitude enveloped her like a heavy cloak, suffocating and oppressive.

"How can I bear this separation?" she murmured, closing her eyes against the sting of fresh tears. It was as if the universe conspired to keep them apart, an unseen hand pulling strings of fate that bound her to a future devoid of love. Her mind raced with thoughts unbidden: Was she truly worthy of his affection? Would she forever remain an unfulfilled dream in the tapestry of his life?

A rustle from her desk drew her attention, forcing her back to the present. There, beneath the scattered remnants of her correspondence, lay the letter from Lady Haine—Reggie's mother. The parchment appeared innocuous enough, yet it held a power that both terrified and intrigued her. She approached the desk, her breath catching as she reached for it. Her fingers trembled, the delicate paper crinkling at her touch.

"Please, let there be something of comfort within," she whispered, clutching the letter tightly as though it were a lifeline. The inked words upon it promised solace, a fleeting hope nestled within the folds of her despair. With resolve, she unfolded it slowly, careful not to mar its pristine edges.

"Perhaps therein lies the key to my happiness," she thought, her heart racing as she prepared to unveil the sentiments penned by a woman who understood the complexities of love and obligation. As she read the familiar script, each loop and swirl ignited a flicker of anticipation within her. She could almost hear Lady Haine's voice guiding her through the words, urging her to fight for what truly mattered.

Dear Juliana,

It began, and with that simple salutation, the world outside faded further, leaving only the pulsing rhythm of her heart and the ink that danced before her eyes. In that moment, she felt the weight of uncertainty lift, replaced by an insistent yearning—the need to reach for Reggie and the love that tethered them together, no matter the obstacles that threatened to sever their bond.

Reginald has always regarded you with admiration.

The truth of those words struck her like a thunderclap, reverberating through the hollow chambers of her heart.

He speaks often of your grace and intelligence.

Those very traits she had feared rendered her unworthy now served as a bridge to his affections—a path she had not dared to tread until this moment.

Though societal expectations weigh heavily upon him, he remains steadfast in his feelings for you.

A fresh wave of warmth coursed through her, dispelling the chill that had settled in her bones. She could envision Reggie's piercing green eyes, that familiar glimmer dancing within them when they shared laughter, the way he leaned just a fraction closer when their hands brushed during heated conversations.

Fight for your love, dear one.

The letter concluded, urging her to seize the day with an unyielding spirit. The final words echoed in her mind, a clarion call that roused her from despair.

She closed her eyes, clutching the letter to her chest, the paper crinkling beneath her grip. This was not merely a missive; it was a lifeline, extending beyond the confines of societal constraints. Juliana's resolve solidified, transforming her heartache into defiance. She would not cower behind propriety and fear.

No longer would she linger in the safety of silence. Juliana stepped forward, her heart a wild drumbeat in her chest, ready to confront the man who held her affections captive. She would unveil her emotions, strip away the barriers of misunderstanding, and finally claim what was rightfully theirs: a love worth fighting for.

With a quick swipe of her delicate hand, Juliana brushed away the remnants of her tears. The cool fabric of her handkerchief felt foreign against her damp skin, yet it was a welcome distraction from the tempest brewing within. She inhaled deeply, filling her lungs with the musty air of the room, and exhaled slowly, allowing the last vestiges of despair to escape along with it.

"Enough," she murmured to herself, straightening her posture as though preparing for a ballroom dance. Each breath steadied the tremors of uncertainty that had plagued her moments before. She was resolute now—no longer a captive of heartache, but a woman determined to seize her destiny.

As she opened the door, the sprawling expanse of the Langdon estate unfolded before her, its grand hallways echoing with the whispers of generations past. Shadows danced in the flickering candlelight, lending an air of solemnity to the otherwise opulent surroundings. Her footsteps sounded firm against the polished wood floors, each step a declaration of her intent.

The portraits lining the walls loomed large, their gilded frames encasing the visages of ancestors long departed. They gazed down upon her, their expressions stoic yet strangely alive, as if they sensed the weight of her emotions. Juliana paused before one such portrait—a great-aunt known for her scandalous elopement. A flicker of a smile tugged at the corner of Juliana's lips. Perhaps she drew strength from the legacy of audacity that coursed through her blood.

"Do not falter, dear Juliana," she whispered, channeling the spirit of her ancestor. "You are made of braver stuff."

With renewed vigor, she pressed on, her mind focused solely on Reggie. Every thought of him ignited a fire within, burning away the doubts that sought to ensnare her resolve. She envisioned his face—the way his eyes sparkled when he laughed, the gentle curve of his smile that had the power to dispel even the darkest clouds. It was this image that propelled her forward, guiding her through the labyrinthine halls towards the promise of love.

As she passed beneath the watchful gaze of her forebears, the air thickened with a sense of purpose. Juliana could almost hear their silent encouragement, urging her to claim what was rightfully hers. She lifted her chin, the determination radiating from her. Tonight, she would confront the man who haunted her every waking thought and declare her heart's truth.

"Tonight, everything changes," she vowed softly, her voice barely above a whisper, yet ringing clear in the silence around her.

Thirteen

THE NEXT DAY

Juliana's fingers trembled as she unfolded the letter, the faint scent of lavender wafting from the parchment. Her heart raced, each beat echoing in her ears like a distant drumroll heralding calamity. The elegant script danced before her eyes, but the words—*"broken off his engagement"*—seared into her consciousness with an intensity that left her breathless.

> *Reggie has broken off his engagement to Lady Meredith,*

She read aloud, her voice barely above a whisper. The world around her faded; the plush sitting room, adorned with delicate china and embroidered cushions, became a blur. Shock coursed through her veins like wildfire, igniting a flicker of hope amid the encroaching shadows of disbelief. *Could it be true? A single thought pressed against her mind: Was this the moment she had longed for, or merely a cruel jest of fate?*

Juliana pressed her lips together, struggling to quell the tumult within. *This was yesterday, why hadn't he come to see her?* Dread coiled tightly in her stomach. *What if he did not feel the same? What if he had changed his mind? What if the bond they shared was merely a childhood folly, destined to fade like summer blooms?*

"Prepare my carriage at once!" she commanded, her voice regaining its usual steadiness. The fire ignited within, dispelling the lingering tendrils of uncertainty. This was no time for hesitation; she would seize this opportunity to confront Reggie, to unveil the feelings she had sheltered for too long.

"Immediately, my lady?" The butler raised an eyebrow, a hint of surprise etched on his features.

"Yes, immediately! There is no moment to lose." Juliana's resolve solidified, her pulse quickening with each tick of the clock. She could no longer wait for fate to dictate her path. It was time to act, to lay bare her heart before the only man who had ever truly understood her.

As she turned from the window, her auburn hair catching the light like spun gold, determination surged within her. She would not allow the whims of society to dictate her happiness any longer. With each step towards the door, her mind raced, crafting the words she would say when she finally stood before him. Would she confess her longing? Would she dare to dream of a future entwined with his?

"Your carriage awaits, my lady," the butler announced, his voice steady despite the urgency of the moment.

"Then let us not tarry!" she replied, her tone resolute. With one final glance at the letter crumpled in her hand, Juliana stepped outside, where the chill of the autumn air invigorated her senses. Each breath filled her with possibility as the coachman bowed respectfully, ready to whisk her away towards a destiny that awaited her just beyond the horizon.

With a quickened breath, Juliana swung the carriage door open and slipped inside, her heart pounding like the hooves of a galloping horse. The plush seat enveloped her as she settled in, but the comfort was lost on her; urgency coursed through her veins. She gripped the edges of her skirts, her knuckles white against the delicate fabric. Every tick of the clock echoed in her mind, a reminder that time could not be wasted.

"To Messingham House, post haste!" she commanded, her voice steady despite the whirlwind of emotions threatening to engulf her. The coachman nodded, his brow furrowed with understanding and flicked the reins. With a jolt, the carriage lurched forward, the wheels rattling over the cobblestones with an insistent rhythm.

As they sped away from her estate, the world outside blurred into a haze of autumn colors, each passing tree and building a mere phantom of her former life. Juliana pressed her palms against her skirts, feeling the faint tremor of anticipation beneath her composed exterior. *How many times had she imagined this moment? How many nights had she lain awake, dreaming of what could be if only fortune smiled upon them?*

The distance between her and Reggie shrank with each turn of the wheels, yet her thoughts remained a tempest. *Would he welcome her with open arms, or would uncertainty linger in his emerald eyes?* She recalled the warmth of their shared laughter, the fleeting glances that spoke volumes, and the unacknowledged affection that had woven its way between them like ivy on a trellis.

"Reggie," she murmured, his name a silent prayer on her lips. The closer they drew to his estate, the more tangible her longing became—a magnetic pull that urged her to leap from the confines of societal restraint. This was her chance, and she would seize it with both hands, for love was worth every risk, every scandalous whisper that might follow in its wake.

The carriage jolted to an abrupt halt, the sudden stop sending Juliana's heart leaping into her throat. Her breath hitched as she peered through the window, eyes widening in disbelief. There, blocking her path, stood Reggie's handsome carriage, its polished exterior gleaming in the afternoon sun like a beacon of hope.

"Reggie," she breathed, a thrill coursing through her veins, igniting every nerve ending. The very air felt charged with possibility, and an exhilarating heat spread from her core, enveloping her entirely. *Had he truly intercepted her, or was this merely a figment of her yearning imagination?*

Before she could gain her composure, the door to his carriage swung open, revealing him in all his dashing glory. He emerged with a grace that seemed to defy gravity, tall and poised, his dark hair tousled by the wind, framing that familiar face she had long admired. Their gazes collided, a spark igniting the space between them, thick with unspoken emotions.

Her heart raced, each beat echoing in her ears as she took in the intensity of Reggie's expression. Those piercing green eyes, usually so charmingly playful, now held a seriousness that made her pulse quicken. In that instant, it was as if the very fabric of their lives interwove, threading together their hopes and fears—a tapestry they had woven over years of friendship, now rendered fragile and exquisite in its vulnerability.

In that charged atmosphere, every secret, every longing they'd harbored surged forth, dancing on the precipice of revelation. Juliana's mind whirled with possibilities, each one more thrilling than the last. *Would he finally acknowledge what had lain dormant for far too long?* The thought sent shivers down her spine, urging her to lean into the unfolding drama before them.

Reggie strode forward with purpose, his long coat flaring behind him as he approached the carriage like a tempest unleashed. The cobblestones crunched beneath his polished boots, each step resonating with a determination that sent a thrill through Juliana's veins. Her breath quickened, a flutter of anticipation twisting in her stomach as she watched him draw nearer.

"Juliana," he said, his voice steady yet laced with an urgency that tugged at her heart. Those piercing green eyes, usually so playful, now bore into her with an intensity that left no room for pretense. "I must speak with you—now."

In that moment, the world around them faded, leaving only the two of them suspended in an atmosphere thick with unspoken desires. She felt the weight of his gaze, a silent declaration that ignited something deep within her—a flicker of hope battling against the years of uncertainty.

"Reggie..." The name escaped her lips in a hushed whisper, a plea, a question.

"Juliana," he interrupted, stepping closer still, his expression resolute. "I have come to realize that my heart has belonged to you all along. I love you. No more can I deny it."

His confession hung in the air, electrifying and profound, sending a tremor through her core. A rush of emotions surged within her—relief, joy, disbelief—all colliding in a kaleidoscope of feeling that threatened to overwhelm her senses. She grasped the edges of her skirts tightly, as if anchoring herself against the tide of revelation.

"Is it true?" she managed to utter, her voice trembling with both hope and trepidation. *Could it be that the love she had harbored in silence mirrored his own?*

"More real than anything I have ever known," he replied, his eyes unwavering, earnest and fierce.

With those words, the dam of restraint shattered, and the truth coursed through her veins, awakening every dormant desire she had buried beneath layers of propriety. A smile broke free, radiant and unguarded, illuminating her face as their hearts intertwined in a moment that transcended the confines of societal expectations.

"Then let us not waste another moment," she breathed, the weight of fear lifted, replaced by the exhilarating promise of love unconfined.

With a heart racing like the thundering of hooves on cobblestones, Juliana inhaled sharply, her resolve solidifying in that charged moment. She grasped the handle of her carriage door, feeling the cool metal beneath her fingers as she pushed it open. The world around them narrowed to the space between herself and Reggie, where anticipation hung thick in the air.

Stepping down onto the uneven ground, her gaze locked onto his. Each footfall felt like a pulse echoing through her body, a magnetic pull drawing her closer. Time seemed to suspend itself; the cacophony of the bustling road faded into a distant murmur. All that remained was the crackling energy electrifying the space between them—a force both thrilling and terrifying.

"Reggie," she breathed, her voice a mere whisper but laden with the weight of unspoken truths. It was as if the very air shimmered with their shared history, the laughter of childhood mingled with whispered dreams of love.

He halted before her, his green eyes gleaming with an intensity that sent shivers along her spine. The world fell away until only they existed within this tender cocoon of understanding. The breath caught in her throat, as though she were suspended on the precipice of something magnificent, something life-altering.

Reggie stepped forward, closing the distance until they were mere inches apart. His hand rose, tentative yet filled with purpose, and cupped her cheek with a gentleness that belied his formidable stature. The warmth of his palm ignited a spark, sending a cascade of sensations racing through her—

an exquisite blend of exhilaration and vulnerability. A profound stillness enveloped them, each heartbeat resonating in the silence that wrapped around their bodies like a silken shroud.

"Juliana," he murmured, his voice low and sincere, reverberating through her very being as he leaned closer. The world beyond them blurred, leaving only the intoxicating reality of their closeness. She could feel the warmth radiating from him, inviting her into a realm where nothing else mattered but the two of them.

"Your touch..." she whispered, her breath quickening, as a delightful tremor coursed through her. It was a truth long buried under layers of decorum, now laid bare beneath the scrutiny of his gaze. The corners of his mouth turned upwards slightly, a hint of a smile mingling with the depth of emotion in his eyes, as though he understood the impact of such tenderness.

"Everything about you captivates me," he said softly, his thumb brushing against her skin, igniting a fire that spread through her veins like wildfire. "It always has."

In that moment, surrounded by the remnants of their past and the promises of a future unfurling before them, Juliana surrendered to the undeniable connection that tethered their hearts together.

Juliana's breath caught in her throat as Reggie's lips descended upon hers, the world around them dissolving into a haze of sensation. The kiss ignited with an intensity that took her by surprise, each soft press and lingering caress weaving together strands of unspoken desire that had long been buried beneath layers of propriety and restraint.

Time itself seemed to falter, stretching into eternity as they lost themselves in the warmth and urgency of one another. His lips moved against hers with a fervor that sent tremors racing through her, awakening every nerve ending, every timid hope she had ever harbored for this very moment. She felt the gentle pull of his hands at her waist, drawing her closer as if he sought to merge their very beings into one.

Reggie tasted of longing and sweet desperation, a promise of what lay within the depths of his heart. As their kiss deepened, she surrendered completely, letting go of the expectations and fears that had shadowed their relationship for so long. In this embrace, nothing else mattered—the scandalous whispers of society, the judgmental gazes of their peers—they were simply Juliana and Reggie, two souls entwined by fate.

As the kiss finally broke, they lingered mere inches apart, breathless. Juliana's heart raced, a wild rhythm echoing in her ears as her gaze locked onto Reggie's intense green eyes. There was a flicker of something profound between them, an understanding that transcended words. It was in the way his brow furrowed slightly, as if he were gathering courage; in the way her pulse quickened under his unwavering stare.

"Juliana," he breathed, the sound heavy with meaning. An unspoken promise hung in the air, a vow etched into the fabric of their connection—a commitment to face whatever awaited them together. In that moment, she understood that the bond they shared was no longer confined to childhood affection or friendship; it was a fierce, undeniable love that demanded acknowledgment.

"Reggie," she replied softly, her voice barely above a whisper yet laden with conviction. A smile spread across his lips, illuminating the shadows that had clouded their hearts for far too long. They stood on the precipice of an extraordinary journey, their futures now intertwined, each heartbeat resonating with the thrill of new beginnings.

In that fleeting moment, before the world rushed back in, they grasped the magnitude of their choice—the willingness to embrace a love that defied all odds, united against the constraints of expectation. And in that silence, as they beheld one another, they knew their hearts would never again walk separate paths.

Epilogue

TEN YEARS LATER

The drawing room, a symphony of soft laughter and playful shrieks, shimmered with the glow of afternoon light filtering through the tall windows. Her Grace, the Duchess of Messingham, her auburn hair catching the sun's rays like molten copper, stood poised at the center of the room. With a mischievous smile gracing her lips, she glanced at Reggie, whose green eyes sparkled with encouragement.

"Watch closely, my dears!" she announced, adopting an elegant stance. The children bounced in their seats, eyes wide with anticipation, while Reggie leaned back against the plush upholstery, feigning indifference but unable to suppress his grin.

With a delicate arch of her neck, Juliana began to mimic the graceful movements of a swan gliding across a lake. She swept her arms wide, curving them gracefully as if cutting through water, her fingers fluttering like feathers. The room erupted into giggles as her youngest, a cherubic boy with unruly curls, squealed with delight.

"Is it a bird? A duck?" he shouted, his small hands clapping together in excitement.

"Close, but not quite!" Juliana replied, her voice lilting with playful challenge. She dipped low, then rose fluidly, embodying the very essence of the majestic creature.

"Ah! I know!" piped up her eldest daughter, her brow furrowed in concentration. "A swan!"

"Correct!" Juliana declared, her laughter mingling with the children's joyous noise. She felt a warm swell of pride as their faces lit up with triumph. Their gleeful camaraderie wrapped around her like a comforting quilt, reminding her of the love that bound their little family together.

Reggie's gaze never left her, admiration evident in the way his lips curled into a soft smile. He relished each moment, watching his wife with the same enchantment as their children. How effortlessly she commanded the room, igniting laughter and wonder with every gesture!

"Your turn, darling," she beckoned playfully, tilting her head toward him, her eyes sparkling with mischief.

"Very well, but I shall have to outdo you," he replied, rising with a theatrical flourish. The children cheered, their voices rising in a delightful cacophony that echoed off the walls adorned with portraits of ancestors long passed.

As Reggie took his place before them, Juliana's heart fluttered. In this vibrant bubble of familial joy, the world outside faded away, leaving only the warmth of their laughter and the sweet innocence of their children's spirits.

Reggie leaned closer to Lady Juliana, the rich warmth of their laughter still lingering in the air. With a conspiratorial smile, he whispered, "I must confess, my love, you have outdone yourself this afternoon." His breath brushed against her ear, igniting a flutter of delight within her.

Juliana turned slightly, her blue eyes sparkling with mischief. "Oh? And what is it that I have accomplished so splendidly?" she teased, tilting her head to catch his gaze.

He wrapped his hand around hers, their fingers entwining effortlessly. "Look at our children," he murmured, gesturing subtly toward their offspring, who were now bubbling over with energy. "This beautiful family we have created together—how did I ever deserve such happiness?"

A wave of warmth enveloped Juliana at his words, and her heart swelled. She could hardly believe how far they had come, from the initial whispers of courtship to the joyful chaos that filled their drawing room. Yes, they had faced challenges, but here they were, surrounded by laughter and love. "We have built something extraordinary, haven't we?" she replied softly, her voice laced with affection.

As if sensing the tender moment shared between their parents, the children began tugging at their sleeves, eager to reclaim the focus. Her youngest son, a whirlwind of curls and exuberance, exclaimed, "Mama! Papa! Watch me!"

"Me too!" piped up her daughter, bouncing on her toes with uncontainable excitement. The other two joined in, a chorus of pleas for attention cascading through the air. Each little face was alight with anticipation, their innocent enthusiasm infectious.

Juliana's laughter rang out, light and free. "It seems we have an audience demanding our attention," she noted, shaking her head with mock seriousness. "What shall we do, my lord?"

Reggie chuckled, his green eyes brightening as he looked at their children. "Perhaps we should give them a turn at charades as well," he proposed, raising an eyebrow playfully. "After all, we wouldn't want to disappoint such eager performers."

"Charades!" the children echoed, their voices blending into a symphony of joy. Their hands flailed excitedly, each one vying for a chance to be the next star of the game.

The couple exchanged an indulgent glance, their hearts brimming with warmth as they embraced the delightful chaos. In that instant, under the soft glow of the chandelier, surrounded by their children's animated chatter, it became abundantly clear: this was their life, a tapestry woven from love, laughter, and the simple joys of family.

Juliana sprang to her feet, her heart quickening with delight as she beheld the eager faces of her children. With a flourish, she swept her youngest son into her arms, his giggles bubbling forth like effervescent champagne. "Hold tight, my little swan," she teased, placing a kiss atop his tousled curls.

Reggie, ever the playful father, effortlessly hoisted the other three onto his shoulders, their laughter mingling in harmonious disarray. "Onward, brave adventurers!" he declared, puffing out his chest in mock bravado. The children squealed with glee, their small hands clutching at their father's hair and shoulders for balance, as they transformed their grand estate into a kingdom waiting to be explored.

Together, they galloped through the elegant hallways adorned with portraits of ancestors long past, the polished wood floors resonating beneath their footsteps. Juliana led the charge, a beacon of joy, her auburn hair cascading behind her like a banner of festivity. She called back to Reggie, "Keep up, my lord! The swan shall not be outpaced."

"Fear not!" he responded, his voice booming with merriment. "I have the finest steeds known to man!" He pretended to gallop in place, causing the children to erupt in fresh waves of laughter.

The echo of their mirth bounced off the walls, an enchanting symphony that filled the expanse of their home, each note a testament to the life they had built together. As they neared the grand doors leading outside, Juliana felt a flutter of excitement; the world beyond awaited, vibrant and alive.

"To the gardens!" she announced, flinging open the heavy oak doors. A rush of fragrant air greeted them, carrying the scent of blooming roses and freshly mown grass. The golden light of the setting sun bathed everything in a gentle glow, transforming the garden into an ethereal landscape.

"Look, Mama! Look, Papa!" called her daughter, pointing to a cluster of butterflies dancing among the flowers. The children squirmed with impatience, eager to break free from their parents' hold and explore the vastness before them.

With a gentle release, Juliana set her youngest down, watching with a swell of pride as he stumbled forward, then turned back to her, beaming. Reggie lowered his children to the ground, and they scattered like leaves in a breeze, their joyous shouts filling the air as they raced toward the flowerbeds.

"Such freedom, my love," Reggie murmured, stepping beside Juliana. They stood shoulder to shoulder, hearts swelling with affection as they observed their children—little bodies dashing through the greenery, laughter rising like music.

"Indeed," Juliana replied, her eyes sparkling as she took in the scene. "They are vivid reminders of our own adventures."

"May we always keep this spirit alive," he said, intertwining his fingers with hers, the warmth of their bond grounding them amid the chaos.

As the sun dipped lower, casting shadows that danced upon their skin, they felt the weight of gratitude settle over them—a reminder of the life and love they nurtured together. Their gazes lingered on their children, who reveled in the magic of the moment, embodying the very essence of joy and innocence.

Lady Juliana led the way, her laughter ringing like sweet chimes as the children flitted around her, their tiny feet pattering against the cobblestones. The grand oak tree loomed ahead, its gnarled branches offering a welcoming shade from the waning sun. She glanced back at Reggie, whose strong form moved with an easy grace, the embodiment of strength and warmth.

"Do you see that?" she called out, pointing toward the sprawling garden where their children raced each other, arms outstretched like birds preparing to take flight. "They are as wild as the wind itself!"

"Indeed," Reggie replied, a fond smile gracing his lips as he caught up beside her. "There is a certain thrill in their abandon, is there not?"

They reached the oak, and without hesitation, Juliana sank onto the soft grass beneath it, pulling Reggie down beside her. Their fingers intertwined, a natural gesture that spoke volumes of their shared understanding and love. Together, they turned their gaze toward the children, who were now tumbling into a patch of daisies, shrieks of delight echoing in the quiet afternoon.

"Look how they play," Juliana murmured, her heart swelling as she watched her eldest daughter attempt to lead her brothers in a dance, arms flailing dramatically as they fell into fits of giggles. "They remind me so much of us—so full of life and mischief."

"Ah, my dear, I dare say they have your spirit," Reggie teased lightly, glancing at her with a knowing twinkle in his eye. "Yet, I cannot overlook the audacity they possess—clearly inherited from their father."

Juliana chuckled softly, leaning her head against his shoulder, finding comfort in the solidness of him. The warmth of the late afternoon sun filtered through the leaves above, casting playful shadows across their entwined hands.

"Do you remember our first summer here?" she asked, the memories washing over her like a gentle tide. "The nights filled with whispered dreams beneath this very tree?"

"How could I forget?" He turned his face toward her, eyes alight with the glow of remembrance. "We were so naive then, believing we could conquer the world. Yet here we are, navigating the greatest adventure of all—parenthood."

"An adventure fraught with challenges," she replied, her voice softening. "But with every trial, we emerge stronger, do we not? Our bond has withstood storms I once thought insurmountable."

"Indeed, my love," Reggie said, the sincerity in his voice grounding her. "We shall continue to nurture that bond, just as we must nurture these little souls. They will need our guidance and unwavering support as they carve their paths."

"To ensure they grow to be kind and brave," Juliana added, determination threading her words. "I want them to know the world is vast and full of wonder, yet not devoid of compassion."

"Then let us vow to provide them with the love and wisdom we have gathered along our journey," Reggie vowed, squeezing her hand gently. "To create a sanctuary for them—a place where laughter reigns and hearts are free."

Together, they watched their children weave through the garden, blissfully unaware of the responsibilities that awaited them. In that moment, beneath the watchful oak, they found solace in their unity, a quiet promise echoing in the space between them.

As the last rays of sunlight slipped beneath the horizon, painting the sky in hues of orange and lavender, the children began to gravitate toward their parents like moths drawn to a flame. Lady Juliana could see it in the way they yawned, their small faces flushed from the day's rambunctious play.

"Come here, my darlings," she beckoned softly, her arms outstretched. The moment they reached her, she enveloped them in an embrace, feeling the warmth of their bodies against hers. Their giggles faded into soft sighs as they nestled closer, seeking the comfort only a mother could provide. Reggie joined the tableau, wrapping his long arms around the cluster of little ones, forming a protective cocoon that radiated love and safety.

"Did you tire yourselves out, my brave adventurers?" he teased gently, peering down at their sleepy faces. His voice held an affectionate lilt, a blend of humor and warmth that coaxed smiles even in weariness.

"Not tired! Just... resting," protested Henry, the eldest, his eyelids betraying him with their heavy droop. "We need more games tomorrow."

"Tomorrow shall bring new adventures indeed," Juliana replied, her gaze sweeping over each cherubic face. She marveled at the family they had crafted together—a tapestry woven from laughter, joy, and unyielding love.

"Come now," Reggie said, rising slowly and lifting the youngest, little Clara, onto his hip. "It is high time we return to our castle. Who will lead the way?"

"Me!" shouted Oliver, the second boy, darting ahead with exuberance despite his own fatigue.

"Very well, brave knight Oliver," Juliana encouraged, smiling as she took hold of Mia's hand, the middle child whose golden curls caught the last light of day. They followed the determined march of their son, the echoes of their footsteps mingling with the chirping of crickets in the encroaching dusk.

The gardens transformed, shadows lengthening as they traversed the vibrant path leading back to the grand estate. Juliana felt a swell of gratitude; these moments, though fleeting, were etched in her heart forever.

Once inside, they moved with deliberate care—each step resonating with the weight of familial love. Reggie ushered the children toward the staircase. "You must all be very quiet now," he whispered conspiratorially, eliciting a chorus of giggles that echoed off the marble walls.

"Like mice!" Mia squeaked, stifling a laugh behind her small hands.

"Exactly," he grinned, eyes glinting with mischief. At the top of the stairs, Juliana paused, relishing the sight of her husband and children illuminated by the soft glow of candlelight.

One by one, they tucked each child into bed, the sweet scent of lavender wafting through the air as she smoothed the blankets around them.

"Goodnight, my little stars," she murmured, leaning down to

press a kiss to each forehead. "May your dreams be filled with wonder."

"Will you tell us another story tomorrow?" Clara asked, her eyes fluttering closed, the remnants of her energy fading away.

"Of course, my love," Juliana whispered, her heart swelling anew. "A story of knights, and dragons, and all things magical."

Reggie, standing sentinel beside her, placed a gentle hand on her shoulder, their fingers brushing lightly—a shared understanding passing between them, a promise of many tomorrows yet to come.

"Sleep well," he added, his voice low and soothing. And as the last flicker of daylight vanished beyond the windows, Juliana turned away from the children's rooms, knowing they would awaken to a world filled with possibility, love, and the steadfast support of their devoted parents.

LADY JULIANA STEPPED into the sanctuary of their bedroom, the soft glow of flickering candlelight casting dancing shadows against the elegantly adorned walls. The rich scent of beeswax mingled with the faintest hint of lavender, remnants of the evening's earlier warmth still lingering in the air. She turned to find Reggie already loosening the cravat that had so diligently confined his neck throughout the day.

"Do you recall our charade of the swan?" she asked, a playful smile curving her lips as she moved closer, relishing the moment.

"Ah, yes," he replied, his deep voice low and warm. "You nearly eclipsed the creature itself. A fine display of grace, I daresay." His green eyes sparkled with mischief, igniting a familiar flutter in her chest.

With a gentle tug, she pulled him closer, an unspoken invitation hanging between them, drawing them into the intimacy they had cultivated over years. As he shed his waistcoat and trousers, exposing the strong lines of his form, she felt her breath catch—her heart raced, caught in the thrill of their connection.

"Come now, do not linger too long," she teased softly, her auburn hair spilling over her shoulders like molten copper as she began to undress. Each article of clothing fell away, unveiling the delicate fabric of her nightgown, whispering against her skin as she slipped beneath the cool sheets.

Reggie followed suit, sliding in beside her, their bodies instinctively seeking each other's warmth. He wrapped an arm around her, pulling her closer until she nestled comfortably against his side, the rhythmic beating of his heart calming her own.

"Juliana," he whispered, his breath brushing against her ear, sending shivers down her spine, "you have filled my life with such joy. I scarcely believed it possible before you graced me with your love."

"Reggie," she murmured back, her voice barely above a whisper, "in your arms, I am home. You are my anchor amidst the storms of this world."

They exchanged tender glances, the weight of their shared history evident in each lingering look. The trials they had faced together melted away in these moments, leaving only the sweetness of their bond, fortified by the laughter of their children and the quiet strength of their devotion.

"May we always cherish this," he said, his thumb gently tracing the curve of her cheek. "The life we've built, the joy woven through our days."

"Indeed," she replied, the corners of her mouth lifting in affirmation. "Together, we shall face whatever tomorrow brings, hand in hand."

As silence enveloped them, the outside world faded to a distant murmur. They lay entwined, the flickering candles casting a golden hue that seemed to wrap around them like a cocoon.

"Goodnight, my handsome husband," she breathed, leaning in to plant a soft kiss upon his lips, tasting the promise of many more such moments to come.

"Goodnight, my love," he returned, his voice hushed yet full of warmth, as they surrendered to the embrace of slumber. In that sacred space, they found peace—a whispered harmony echoing in the quiet of the night, knowing they had discovered their forever in one another's arms.

THE END

The Surprise Heir

BY TRISHA FUENTES

In the charming era of Regency England, a tale of unexpected love and enduring destinies unfolds. **Edmund Gallagher**, a distant relative to the prestigious Lord of Langston Hall, lives a modest life far removed from the grandeur of his noble kin. His childhood memories of Langston Hall are few, but one delightful memory of climbing a treehouse with the young lord, **Rupert Hargrove**, continues to warm his heart through the years.

Now, decades later, Rupert, hailed as the dashing heir to Langston Hall, is poised to marry the impeccable Miss Abigail Stronghold, securing his personal happiness and a prosperous future for the estate. However, just as wedding bells are to ring, an unforeseen tragedy befalls Rupert, turning Langston Hall upside down.

Equally entrapped by societal expectations and her burgeoning feelings, Miss Stronghold also finds herself at a crossroads. With the stability of Langston Hall and the future of its inhabitants uncertain, will Edmund and Abigail confront the dictates of their class and follow their hearts, or will they forsake personal happiness for the sake of tradition and duty?

This Regency romance weaves a compelling story of love, loss, and the choices that define us.

The Thunderbolt Series - Book 1

Ebook & Paperback

Service Daughter Series

YOUR NEXT SERIES

HARDSHIP SHOULDN'T HAVE TO BE SUCH AN UPHILL BATTLE

Meet Louisa, Caroline & Hannah

Three daughters born into service. Each with their own story to tell and happily ever after. Simple, ordinary and untitled, unnoticed by the wealthy, struggling with how to survive, how to obtain joy...much less a husband.

SERVICE DAUGHTER SERIES

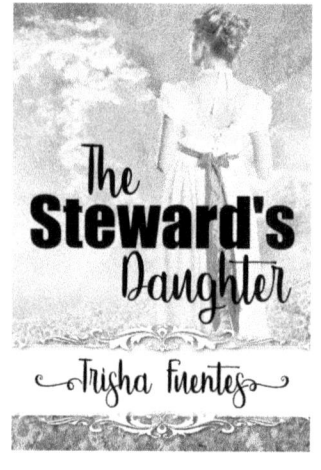

ALL LOUISA WANTED WAS TO BE USEFUL...

The only child of Mr. Ralph Hadley, Land Steward to the Earl of Monbossom, Miss Louisa Hadley lives in a small cottage on the Monbossom estate with her father. When she accidentally breaks her foot after dismounting a horse she is forced to stay in the main house while her father tends to the Earl abroad. With the family now responsible for Louisa's well-being, the classes have reversed as Louisa is constantly scorned by her friends in service. Her circumstances take a more dramatic turn when she stumbles upon the Earl of Monbossom while saving a duckling.

When did he return from France? And who knew his eyes were so blue?

Book 1
Ebook & Paperback

SERVICE DAUGHTER SERIES

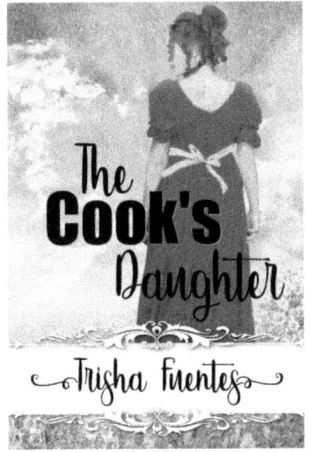

CAN A KITCHEN MAID FIND TRUE HAPPINESS?

Miss Caroline Bates began working in the kitchen with her mother when she was twelve. Caroline grew up with the children of Wellsbury Hall, and watched Lord Gretner's eldest son, Alfred court several noblewomen until one day he finds Caroline practically naked in a nearby moor river.

Is Caroline ruined for all eternity or does she use this mischance to her advantage?

Book 2
Ebook & Paperback

SERVICE DAUGHTER SERIES

WHICH PATH TO FOLLOW?

The only daughter of a curator of St. Anne's Church, Miss Hannah Pickering grew up knowing she was going to become a nun until she is introduced to one of her father's parishioners. Tempted by the handsome widower who attends her father's church, Hannah is suddenly forced to make a worrisome decision.

Book 3
Ebook & Paperback

About Trisha

Hey, it's Trish...

I'm a Romance Author of 39+ books, plus own a Publishing House of 50+ Pen Name Authors.

I've been writing romance with a whole lot of heat lately. I love to write fun, fast romances with witty leading ladies getting that gorgeous, sexy, yet lovable guy that doesn't take months to finish. Happily Ever After with a little bit of love angst in between. Whether you yearn for Historical or Modern, I always have a story for you!

Rejoice, Romance Reader...

For upcoming releases, book news, and other goodies, subscribe to my Newsletter!
https://bit.ly/49BR3UB

- instagram.com/authortrish
- amazon.com/Trisha-Fuentes/e/B002BME1MI
- facebook.com/booksbyTrish
- youtube.com/theardentartist

Also by Trisha Fuentes

✸ Modern Romance ✸

A Sacrifice Play

Faded Dreams

Never Say Forever

* * *

✸ Historical ✸

The Anzan Heir

Magnet & Steele

The Relentless Rogue

One Starry Night

In The Moonlight With You

Captivating the Captain

The Merry Widow

Unrequited Love

The Summer Romance of the Duke

✸ Series ✸

HOLLINGER

Dare To Love - Book 1

A Matchless Match - Book 2

Arrogance & Conceit - Book 3

Impropriety - Book 4

SERVICE • DAUGHTER

The Steward's Daughter - Book 1

The Cook's Daughter - Book 2

The Curator's Daughter - Book 3

THUNDERBOLT

The Surprise Heir - Book 1

A Dance of Deception - Book 2

Win the Heart of a Duchess - Book 3

OBSESSION

Unsuitable Obsession - Part One

Broken Obsession - Part Two

ESCAPE

Swept Away - Book 1

Fire & Rescue - Book 2

The Domain King - Book 3

AGE • GAP • ROMANCE

Whispers of Yesterday - Book 1

His Encore, Her Ecstasy - Book 2

Against the Wind - Book 3